The Rooms Are Filled

The Rooms
Are Filled

a novel

Jessica Null Vealitzek

SHE WRITES PRESS

Published 2014
Printed in the United States of America
ISBN: 978-1-938314-58-2
Library of Congress Control Number: 2013951191

For information, address:
She Writes Press
1563 Solano Ave #546
Berkeley, CA 94707

For Henry & Clara

By wisdom a house is built, and by understanding it is established; by knowledge the rooms are filled with all precious and pleasant riches.

—Proverbs 24:3-4

One

Michael watched the paramedics work on his father. He stared at their backs, black uniforms hiding John Nygaard except for his booted feet, which now rested the same as when he slept in the hammock, toes pointing out. Michael had been in the barn when his mother yelled, milking the cow after school. He ran out and kneeled over his father, who had been mending a rotted fence post just outside the barn door when he collapsed. And then, minutes later, the ambulance cut across the yard, over the patches of snow, and the paramedics circled his father, blocking Michael out. Anne held Michael back and hugged him tight; he could feel her rounded belly behind him. He was jealous, did not want strangers around his father in this moment. John's head lay too near a patch of cold mud, his jeans wet from the slush. They weren't being careful.

He thought of dry pine boughs laid on the ground, like the ones his father laid for him in the forest clearing. He glimpsed his father's limp fingers, dry and cracked white, rolling with each compression, each bit of forced life. Even at nine, Michael knew this was absurd, just one day after Michael's first outing with him, his first visit to his father's clearing in the woods.

John woke Michael early yesterday morning, a Sunday, and Michael knew where they were going. He had always hoped his father would bring him, yet never dared ask. Jumping out of bed, he threw on several layers over his long underwear as his father filled a thermos with coffee in the kitchen. John handed Michael the rifle before they left.

"We're going to Ebersold's first," said John, in response to Michael's questioning look.

Michael followed his father in the snow. The great Minnesota Northwoods grew up around them, black branches piercing the sky in frozen prayer. His bare fingers wrapped around the rifle, one hand on the butt end, one hand on the barrel. It was the same rifle his father taught him to shoot last year at the age of eight, mostly at pop cans in the backyard. He handled and shot a gun expertly now, though he still asked his father to wring the necks of the birds still alive in the tall grass.

The woods were cold and dark. The snow looked blue under the black sky, and the only sound came from their boots crunching snow into ice. Not even the squirrels had scurried down the trees yet. It was the period before dawn when the whole world slept.

After many minutes, the sun's rays scattered through the tree trunks ahead of them. Michael watched the brown plaid of his father's broad back sway side to side, side to side, as he pushed ahead in the snow, dragging along a stick that made a tiny trench beside them. The swaying made Michael dizzy, so he looked away and saw Ebersold's field through the trees to their right, its fresh sheath white except in the middle, where it still soaked red.

John stopped. A piece of bait lay alongside the trail ahead of them. He stabbed around the bait with his stick. A steel trap snapped, and Michael started.

"They laid more," said John. "Let's go." He threw the stick, the trap's teeth clenched on like a dog, into the trees. "Goddamn Ebersold."

Michael had heard it before, how Ebersold had been leaving his sick and butchered cattle in the woods for years, letting wolves clean up his messes. "Then he's angry," John always said, "when those wolves cross an invisible boundary onto his farm and take the food they've developed a taste for." John was known as a radical, and some farmers called him a tree-hugger. He regularly scoured the woods for traps, especially in late fall when wolf pelts were at a prime and therefore the number of wolf traps multiplied, or in spring whenever he heard of the loss of a calf or sheep. John usually left the traps where they were after he tripped them, but sometimes he hid them in hollow trees, forcing the owner to search. He told Michael he felt like a wood sprite, invisible and secret, though the truth was every farmer in four counties knew who was behind the work. Once, a trap had a note taped to it: "Hi, John. Have pity." His father placed the note in his pocket for later storytelling before tripping the trap with a stick and neatly placing it on the side of the trail, careful to brush any dirt from the teeth.

Most farmers were kind to him; they didn't care how softhearted John Nygaard was. And most of them wouldn't have asked the Fish & Wildlife Service to lay traps, as Ebersold did when one of his live-stock was killed two nights ago.

Only a few dozen yards farther, John stopped again. "Damn it."

Michael peeked around his father's body. A wolf lay ahead, its front leg broken in a trap, its huge paw slack. The wolf saw them but did not lift its head. Only its eyes moved from father to son. Plumes of warm breath rose from its nostrils.

"She's probably been out here all night," said John.

Michael looked at her black-tipped ears and spine, the lighter underbelly. "Do you know it?"

"It's the grandmother." John glanced briefly at his son before grabbing the gun.

"Why?" asked Michael, his voice tight.

"They'll euthanize her when they get here. Who knows how long that will be." John moved forward.

"But why don't we try to save her?"

"It's a wild wolf, Michael. The only way we can help her is by shooting her. If you don't want to watch, walk back a hundred yards and I'll come to you." He placed a hand on his son's head. "I thought you were ready."

Michael wanted to be ready. But he did not like that to save the animal, they had to kill it. She wouldn't know he and his father were not like the rest of them.

But she seemed to have been waiting. She watched Michael, and he stared back. A feeling stirred in his belly, at once of longing and being at home.

Michael stayed. He could not take his eyes off the animal. He was still looking when his father shot the gun. There was nothing but the echo across the fields and a flutter of gray fur where the bullet entered. No reflexive movement, no birds in flight. As they walked away, Michael still watched her, calm in the white and red snow.

The paramedics had stopped moving. They were looking at him, at his mother. One of them put his hand on Michael's head, and Michael saw his lips moving. Then they were carrying John to the ambulance, and Michael was walking with his mother to the house.

The two of them stood in the doorway and looked in at their kitchen, at the large old farm table in the center. A yellow-checked kitchen towel lay crumpled in the middle of the table, a block of cheese half cut with a knife still inside it. She'd been preparing lunch when she looked out the window and saw John on the ground. She'd been about to call out to him to run into town for bread.

"Are you hungry? We need bread," Anne said to Michael, as if it was the oddest thing. How could they still need bread?

Michael watched his mother's eyes dart around the kitchen as she held her stomach with both hands. He watched her breath grow deeper, each one more pronounced than the one before, as if the air might run out. She bent over, then kneeled on the ground. He knelt beside her and threw his arms around her shoulders, holding on as together they heaved up and down with their crying.

Michael's room was cold when he woke. He pulled the quilt up to his chin and contemplated lying in bed a bit longer. But the sun's light was peeking over the curve of the earth, pushing ahead of the sun itself, and Michael knew that soon the farmhouse would be bathed in white sunrise. He needed to gather eggs and lay hay for the draft horse by breakfast. They didn't need the horse—his father owned a tractor—but John had felt sorry for it when its owner, an old bachelor down the road, died and the bank came to sort out and sell what was left.

Michael loved this moment of the day. As he stepped out into the yard, looking to the cold fields and the trees in the distance, this moment felt as if it were his—across the land, across the seas, across the world. His. He imagined the sun warming each living thing, the birds and squirrels and trees, all stretching up from slumber. And he was the only one to witness this waking of living things, as if for the very first time, on the very first day.

When he returned to the house with the eggs, his mother was ready with melted butter in a warm skillet.

"Over easy this morning," she said. "No milk yet. I'm letting your father sleep in a bit."

Michael watched his mother cook, the back of her brown hair slightly wavy and pulled back into a low ponytail. Though she was a small woman, she had the honed muscle of a farm wife. She'd had a scholarship and studied English at the University of Minnesota in the mid 1960s, but after graduation she got married. She devoted herself to taking care of the home and farm and trying to have a baby. Born in farm country, she was happy there.

Michael's father came out of the bedroom pulling on suspenders.

"Morning," he said. "It must be half past seven."

"Quarter to eight," said Anne.

John leaned down to kiss her forehead as she scraped the eggs around the skillet, tendrils of steam rising and dissipating in the sunny kitchen.

Anne looked at him sideways and smiled. "Shall we tell him?" she asked.

"I can't believe you haven't already."

"I was waiting for you."

"Tell me what?" asked Michael.

His parents turned to him. But each was waiting for the other to begin and so the kitchen remained quiet.

"Tell me what?" Michael repeated, moving forward in his seat.

"You're going to be a brother," said Anne, and Michael squealed. John kissed Anne on the cheek, then picked up Michael and swung him in circles until the kitchen became a white and yellow blur.

But that was two days ago, no, three. No, maybe three weeks, or months. Michael couldn't tell, didn't know how to mark the passage of time anymore, could only think of previous moments not in the linear past but in a whole mixed-up sphere that he wanted to sink into the center of and grab hold. Change happens quickly, Michael learned. Suddenly something is true. It wasn't, and now it is.

He pushed the covers off and forced himself up to sitting, placing his bare toes on the cold wood floor. When he entered the kitchen, his mother was at the counter preparing lunch already, a fresh chicken and pickled carrots she'd canned last fall. Breakfast sat on the table.

"Do you want help?" Michael asked.

"No. Just sit and eat."

"Are you feeling better?" This didn't sound right to Michael; it wasn't enough of a question to show all he meant to ask.

"Better." She paused in her work and looked out the window into the morning. Michael could see from her profile that she'd been crying. "I was just noticing the snow on the pines across the road. It's full of meltwater that froze again overnight. Makes it look like clouds all along the branches. Lovely, don't you think?"

Michael looked. "Sure, it's pretty."

She resumed cutting. Harder, he thought. "I don't think there's any place lovelier in the world. I don't ever want to leave it."

A cat scratched at the door and mewed.

"Here," said Anne. "Give her these chicken scraps."

Michael opened the door and leaned down. "Hi, girl." The cat grabbed a piece of skin and trotted away, and as Michael rose he could see his father coming up the walk. John looked tired as he stomped the snow off his boots, but he smiled as he stepped over the threshold past Michael and into the kitchen. He walked up behind his wife and put his arms around her waist as Michael watched. She laid her head back on his shoulder for a moment, then continued cutting the chicken.

"We have to go into town today," said Anne, "to the funeral parlor," and Michael lost sight of his father, saw only his mother still at the counter. She put down the knife and washed her hands at the sink. "Forgive me, Michael," she said, as she walked to him by the door. "I forgot myself." She pulled his head to her chest. "How are you?"

"Okay," he said, but again it wasn't enough.

"Let's go, Michael. I'll let you drive," John would have said.

And Michael would have jumped up into their old, light blue truck and placed the county phone book on the seat so he could see properly. His left leg would get the clutch down just far enough.

As it was, he sat next to his mother and looked out as she drove. The road was hard-packed earth with patches of gravel and ice. They passed the neighboring Mulvey farm with its tall silo, passed the sled hill he raced down on a steel shovel with Pike Mulvey, both boys holding their legs in the air, thigh muscles burning, until they dug in their heels to stop just short of the lake. It was the same lake where, last spring, Pike caught the biggest northern anyone remembered ever seeing. Many thought it was mostly his father's doing, but his father always claimed he'd been down the shore trying to unsnag his line from a willow, hadn't even known Pike—then called Daniel—had a line in the water. How an eight-year-old got such a fighter as a northern onto land was suspect, but then Pike, since the age of five, had won every arm-wrestling match at school and could carry a kitchen cord of wood on his own.

The road upped and dipped over the farm fields like a ribbon for the seven miles to town. Michael had heard this land described as monotonous, but he found a home in every hill and gully. A stand of white pines signaled they were nearing the gas station, followed by the market and the post office. The town was two blocks long, nothing much—the larger town, with the grain elevator and clothing stores, was ten miles beyond—but the funeral parlor was here, as well as a beauty parlor, several bars, and a one-room movie theater that sometimes had current releases.

All of these things were still here. Only his father wasn't. Michael could not reconcile the two facts, could not make them match, and so he felt like he was floating through something that wasn't real. It all should have passed with his father.

Anne pulled over at the post office out of habit, something everyone did no matter his or her errand, something Michael had done with John many Saturdays. He grabbed the door handle but then looked over at his mother. Anne had turned off the truck but held onto the key in the ignition. She stared ahead, and Michael waited for her to move. She restarted the truck, and Michael let go of the handle as they pulled back onto the road. When they arrived at the funeral parlor, she left the truck running to keep him warm. "You wait here, Michael. I'll be a few minutes." But when the heavy oak door closed behind her, Michael scooted over and grabbed the wheel.

The one-story brick post office had a perfectly flat roof that leaked in the middle. Customers were used to walking around a white plastic bucket placed in the center of the room. It was still there, Michael noticed. Still there.

Pike's father, Bob Mulvey, leaned an elbow on the counter and chatted with Mr. Sogard, the clerk. Bob was middle-aged, though something about his eyes made him seem older, a leathery tiredness surrounding shallow blue pools. Always the farmer, he wore denim overalls with his work shirt and mud-splattered boots, his finger-nails caked with dirt, slop, and blood. He was not unique among the men in this area, at once tender and rough, naive and hardened. Men like this surrounded Michael and made him feel safe.

"Michael," said Mr. Mulvey, and he straightened.

The clerk smiled kindly as he passed over a couple of envelopes. Michael grabbed them and turned to go.

"Tell Pike hey," he said over his shoulder, but Mr. Mulvey stopped him with a gentle hand on his arm. "We'll be over again later. Tell your mother."

When Michael returned to the funeral parlor, Anne was still inside. He parked the truck and scooted back over to the passenger seat. Out the window, a cardinal sat on a telephone wire, piping its hooo-wit. Hoo-wit. Hoo-wit. Hoo-wit. A loud and clear whistle, calling out, calling to. And Michael began to cry, the tears falling like the fast-dripping icicles along the gutter of the funeral parlor. They fell without forethought, almost without knowledge, like the moment just after his father's death. Just yesterday, but how could that be? His mother emerged, squinting in the sunlight, and pulled her old wool coat around her growing belly. When she opened the door and saw Michael sitting in his tears, looking at her for help, she stepped up and pulled him to her, his nine-year-old legs trailing behind him.

It was late afternoon by the time they drove up their gravel drive-way, the white farmhouse coming into view between the pines and bare oaks. Michael usually had chores before dinner, and he wanted to do them. He stacked the wood his father chopped yesterday morn-ing and salted the walkways between the house and outbuildings so the melting snow wouldn't freeze overnight. He raked the chicken yard and set aside the extra corn he found for the squirrels. He imagined the purple silhouettes of his father and Mr. Mulvey in the fields, discussing where and what to plant come spring.

When the funeral and visitations were over, when pie was eaten and stories told, frozen casseroles wrapped and placed in the freezer, and sorry visitors trickled to none, Michael's mother sat him down at the kitchen table. "We have to move," she said.

No, Michael thought. *No. No. No.* "We can't," he said. "We can't move. This is our farm."

"Yes, but we have to leave it."

He shook his head. "This is our farm! You can't make me do this, too!"

"We'll have a new house, in Illinois. A town called Ackerman—where your Uncle Kevin lives."

"I don't care. We don't have to go." He kicked his foot again and again under the table.

"Yes, Michael, we do. I have to work. Kevin's hired me as a waitress."

Michael looked at his mother then, his quiet and strong and schooled mother. She could never wear some silly outfit. She could never take orders on a notepad.

"We'll leave by August, in time for you to start fourth grade."

"I'm not going." He believed this. He would find a way. "I'll stay with Pike."

"We can't survive otherwise. We'll barely have anything left after paying off the mortgage. Things will be tight, but better than here."

"Nothing's better than here." He kicked harder and hoped he'd find her leg.

Anne placed a hand over his. "There's no way around this. We'll have to go through."

Michael saw that her eyes were wet and that she was about to cry, but he ran to the barn and left her sitting at the table. He stroked the cow's neck and talked to his father, still so present in his life that he could hear his words, his voice. He saw his father rub his eyebrow and pick at the hairs as he broached the tender subject.

"She already found a nice little house to rent," his father said. "You might like it."

He looked away. "You know I'm not going to like it."

"I know you, Michael. I know you'll be alright."

"What about the cat?"

"The neighbors will feed her."

"Who'll take care of the animals?"

"The new people will buy them."

Michael watched the cow and the horse in the stall beside it and envied them. They were home and always would be.

"Why does someone else get to live here and not us!" he cried. He could hear his father, could see him, but could not run to him as he so wanted. He laid his head against the cow but pushed his cheek too hard, so the cow sidestepped and Michael stood upright again. "What about the wolves? Who'll find the traps?"

"It's been troubling me, too, Michael. But wolves have been around far longer than we have. They'll make it far after, I suspect."

"Stop it! You don't want us to leave!"

His father only said, "There's nothing left to do."

Michael dropped down into the hay and grabbed a bunch in both fists. "I'm not leaving you."

"You don't have to." His father moved closer, and Michael believed for a second that he could touch him.

"You're coming?"

"Wherever you go."

Michael could almost feel him, his face turned up toward the wide barn doors and the warm outside. He closed his eyes so he could imagine hugging him.

"Your mother lost me same as you," his father said. "Don't be hard on her."

For weeks after, whenever he was not at school, Michael sat in the barn. He watched his house, a thing he knew was wood and nails, but he wanted to hug it, wrap his arms around the large chimney his father had built before Michael was born, hauling rocks up from the lake. He wanted to hug the front steps where his father and mother used to sit talking, dark shadows against the white house, while he caught lightning bugs in the yard. Michael wanted to hug the doors that led to hard-packed earth in the cool cellar, his favorite place on humid summer days. His friends were scared there might be ghosts, but not Michael.

He looked at the fields behind the house, the trees beyond, and the lake he knew was after that. His mother had said their new home was in a suburb, with many houses side by side on every street. They would have a yard, though she did not know how big. She worried whether she could have a garden.

"I'll come visit," said Pike one Saturday as the end of the school year approached. They'd planned on riding bikes to town, the day being the kind of sunny that warms without causing sweat. But the move was too imminent, and Michael could not bear to spend even one afternoon away from home. So they played catch in the back-yard between the house and barn, in the shade of an oak tree. The farm cat sat atop the picnic table and watched. As Michael caught the ball, he tried not to look at the rotting fence post next to the barn behind Pike.

"Will you?" asked Michael.

"Sure. I can get my dad to drive me. Or maybe there's a train from Minneapolis."

"I'm sure there's a train. Or a bus."

"I'll come," said Pike.

On a warm day in May, Michael came home from school to find Mr. Mulvey sitting on the front step, elbows on his knees. He twirled a long stem of grass in his fingers. Michael sat down next to him on the old wood and watched a garter snake disappear under the house. He liked it when Mr. or Mrs. Mulvey stopped by to visit; he liked anyone who had known his father.

"Your mother had a miscarriage," said Mr. Mulvey. "The baby's gone."

The baby had not yet come, so Michael could not imagine it being gone. He understood that now there was no chance of the baby, that it would not come at all, and he remembered that he'd planned to tell it about the wolves, would have had to because the baby would never have known Minnesota, or their father. This gave him a twinge of ache in his heart, but the loss felt so much smaller than the loss of his father. It was nothing compared to that. And so it didn't hurt, not really. That made him feel better.

Michael didn't want to say that, didn't know what to say, but he knew Mr. Mulvey didn't expect him to say anything. They sat in silence awhile until Michael remembered to ask about his mother.

"Is she okay?"

Mr. Mulvey looked down at his hands. "About okay as you'd expect, I guess."

Anne had been unprepared for the question.

She filled out the forms a nurse had brought her, and on automatic she wrote in her name, age, address, insurance. She signed waivers for the dilation and evacuation she was about to receive. And then, sandwiched in the middle of the mundane, she was asked what she wanted to do with the baby's remains. The hospital would dispose of them at her wish, or she could bring them home for burial.

Why hadn't she thought of this? Of course she should have thought of it. She had been almost five months pregnant. She had felt the baby move. Why had she not thought of this?

Out of habit, she reached for the phone to call John but then pulled back into sobs. A nurse brought her water and tissues but then had no words, knew there were none, and having witnessed many tragedies was not self-conscious about it. She touched Anne's shoulder before leaving the room. Anne placed her hands on her abdomen and closed her eyes, hugging the baby with her mind and blood and being, loving the piece of John she carried. She cried until the tears were gone from her, and then opened her eyes. Her pain—her intense, heaving pain— had already killed her baby. She could not let it do any more harm. She wouldn't let it. She'd do better for Michael.

The baby was a girl, they learned afterward, and Michael stood at Anne's bedside and asked if they could name her Diane. "After the song dad always sang," he said. "I can't get it out of my head."

Anne knew then that they would bury her—just she and Michael and Mr. Mulvey leaning against a shovel in the backyard, standing in the sun. Surrounded by trees and grass and sky, and all the things that would remain. It was the right place for her.

Later, when Mr. Mulvey left and they sat on the grass, Anne grabbed Michael's face in her hands and watched him for several moments, rubbing his cheeks with her thumbs. His hair and eyes were the deep brown of wet tree trunks. Behind them, inside, boxes of clothes and dishes, books and knickknacks, filled the living room in crooked towers. "I couldn't have raised two children on my own," she finally said, but that was all.

The sun burned through July. Michael wished hard and felt hopeful to the end, but the day came, as any day. He and his mother packed up the truck and trailer one morning and said goodbye to their farm, to the places of his father, to the baby. Before he left the house for good, Michael snuck a knife from a box and pushed it hard into the front door jamb. It felt good as he broke through the grain and scratched out the letters. *Michael 1983.* If he could not take it with him, he would leave something behind.

Two

Julia Parnell gripped the steering wheel as though it kept her from falling out of the car and rolling down the highway. She thought if she let go or stopped the car she might never start again, and so she drove and drove, right out of Iowa. She knew where she was headed but did not trust herself to get there. And so she held on, hands sweating, forehead sweating, back sweating, because the air conditioner in her car would not blow cold.

The swollen late-summer trees along the highway moved in the prairie breeze. Corn was her friend here, rows of green present and dependable. Dependably quiet.

She turned off the radio because every song had too much meaning. When she hit Dubuque, she stopped for gas but entered the full-service line so she would not have to leave the car. And still, her hands gripped the wheel. As she crossed the Mississippi River into Illinois and entered gently rolling hills, she calmed. In Galena, she pulled off the road and parked near a fruit and vegetable stand, enjoying the company of strangers as she sat on the hood of her car in the gravel parking lot and again began the letter she knew she had to write.

August 15, 1983
Dear Rose,
I hurt. And I know it's my doing.

But once again, she couldn't finish. The few words she could think of sounded weak. The rest were mixed up in her head and wound together so tightly she didn't know what the words were or how to untangle them.

She balled up the paper and threw it into a metal bin next to the fruit tent. The cashier smiled at her. It was a nice smile, well meant, but it reminded Julia of her mother. Maybe she would have thought of her anyway, that omnipresent being standing somewhere above Julia's head and noticing all things. Noticing and knowing. Smiling, but not meaning well.

She would love this, thought Julia, *me sitting in the middle of nowhere. Right through her smile she would be able to reach with invisible claws and gut me. Well, that's a bit dramatic. And not.*

The only time Julia remembered her mother actually yelling was when the dog vomited on the new ivory carpet. Mrs. Parnell was expecting the bridge club any minute, and the smell was suffocating, not to mention the orange stain in the middle of the living room among the card tables. When she screamed at the dog, spit flew from her mouth, and Julia was scared she might kick it. The dog had interfered with Mrs. Parnell's golden rule: Do unto others whatever you must to make them feel comfortable and at ease. Her bridge club would certainly feel awkward trying to hold pleasant conversation while the sour smell of bile and kibble clung to the air.

Her mother must have yelled other times, but Julia did not remember. She always seemed to know what she must do to avoid the treatment given the dog, which was not allowed out of the parameters of the tile kitchen for six years except to relieve itself or take a brief walk. Julia learned to laugh at jokes she did not understand and agree with opinions she did not share. When she was older, Julia often pretended to not comprehend something if it gave someone pleasure to explain it to her, especially a man.

Julia pleased. But Rose, her lifelong friend, was asking her to do something she simply could not do. And while Julia could blame it all on the way her mother raised her, in truth, she shared her mother's philosophies. Making others uncomfortable pained her; their disappointment caused *her* to squirm in shame. She remembered an incident in high school when she was a faceless member of the large student body government. She attended all the meetings, listening from her seat in the middle of the others in the auditorium. Sometimes she had the urge to speak about some issue or another, but her chest would fill with what felt like a thousand tiny pellets and they would rise to her throat and then her face, causing it to burn red. She never spoke.

But one day, the first warm day of spring, most of the students skipped the meeting and headed for lunch outside. Julia sat among a handful of other members as the president called the meeting to order from the front of the room. Toward the end, when the president asked whether there was any other business, a girl Julia did not know raised her hand and stood.

"I'd like to propose that the student body government sign a petition demanding the ban of *Forever* in our school library," she said.

A few students murmured, and Julia could not tell if it was approval or disapproval. She had only heard of the book; she had not read it.

"It's filth that I believe is best left to the trash bin or the homes of pedophiles," said the student.

The president looked hesitant. "What's in it?" she asked.

"Sex. Pornography." The girl looked around the room, adding, "The *pill.*"

"Pornography?" asked the president.

The girl nodded. "It's disgusting."

Julia slowly raised her hand as she said, "Does it matter?"

The girl turned Julia's way. "Excuse me?"

Julia remained seated. "I mean, aren't we supposed to not ban books? Does it matter what they're about?"

Irritated, the girl said, "What are you talking about?"

"We were just reading about Hitler in World History. He burned books. Aren't we supposed to not be like Hitler?"

The girl rolled her eyes. "That's different."

"Why?"

The girl spoke succinctly, as if explaining something to a little sister. "This is a book about sex and birth control being available in a library for students, some who are only fourteen years old."

Julia was not exactly comfortable, but she felt armed with Mr. Rudolph's lesson last period on the danger of a society where thought and expression were policed. She stood, warming to this feeling of speaking up and out. "But if we start—"

"Whatever." The president interrupted Julia, who immediately sat back down. "This is annoying and it's the end of the period. Let's vote."

Julia left defeated.

Sitting on the hood of her car, she was able to recall the humiliation instantly. She knew it might not have bothered others, but it bothered her. And she was okay with that. It's who she was. She didn't want to change the world, though later, sitting on the bus on the way home, she did plan to recount the story to her mother, hoping for her delighted surprise at Julia's courage and the "My word!" she often offered her friends when they accomplished a delicious pie or organized a particularly lovely party.

Julia slid off the hood and got into the car. Her sweat-soaked shirt felt cool against her back, for a moment. Then the heat penetrated from the blue vinyl cushion. She sat, flushed, and the cashier appeared at her window.

"You all right?" she asked, her apple cheeks striped with sweat sliding down from her hairline.

"Oh, yes, sorry. I'm fine. Just a little hot."

The cashier passed a pint of raspberries into the car. "Here. Good and juicy."

"Oh, thanks, I couldn't."

She placed them on her lap. "Sure you could."

Julia reached for her purse. "I'm not sure I have . . . How much are they?"

"Just take them. Go on now. Safe travels." She backed away from the car.

Julia smiled, overcome with guilt. "Thank you," she said, and out of habit she thought of a way to repay the cashier for her kindness.

"Will 20 get me to Ackerman Road?" she asked, though she knew it would not.

The cashier shook her head. "Oh honey, no. You gotta jump on 90 down a ways. That goes straight through to Chicago. Just hop off where the sign says Ackerman."

Three

The Nygaards' new ranch home was a rare exception in a neighborhood in which most houses were built in the same Colonial style during the same three months of the same year, 1958, by the same developer who bought the land from a farmer named Miles Hausmann. The Hausmann family had owned the land for four generations, milking their cows and sending the dairy on the Illinois & Wisconsin Railroad twenty miles southeast to Chicago. Miles got older, though, and was tired of milking cows. He had two children, but both grew up and out, heading to the great big city for great big jobs. At first, Miles sold just a parcel of his land for extra income, and he thought he'd leave it at that. Then he sold another larger parcel, and then another, until finally, by the time Miles died, the rich loam was eaten up by brick and clay, asphalt and rock. When Michael and his mother moved into a house on Miles Hausmann's old land, the original farmhouse still stood nearby, but on only a quarter acre, and the owners of the farmhouse were a retired economics professor and his wife.

The town of Ackerman was founded on a low, flat hill in the 1830s by Methodist farmers who came from New York. The move was the last in a series of westward pushes that started with their ancestors in Germany, moved through Ireland, and landed in America.

The farmers trudged west, away from the rocky soil of the east, swung around the tip of Lake Michigan, past the mud swamp streets of the growing village named Chicago after the Algonquin Indian word for the wild onions that grew along the river there. The farmers came to another river, the Des Plaines. They walked through the water, and on the other side they looked up and saw an endless prairie of tall grass and groves of oak and knew finally that they would stop.

The men and their wives and children called the settlement Ackerman after Andreas Ackermann, who was among them. Andreas was well-liked by the group as well as the local Algonquin tribe who had followed, spied on, and finally visited and traded with the settlers along the way since Lake Michigan. Ackerman was a fitting name, for *ackermann* means "farmer" in German, and these men had come to till the earth and push their seeds into the black loam. The Methodists did not see the need for that second "n," however, and so they dropped it, for the excess bothered them.

The farmers were successful at their trade, and soon they and Chicago merchants convinced the railroad authority to extend a line out to Ackerman. In the 1850s, it was the first and only stop on the northwest line.

Chicago grew and Ackerman grew. Decade by decade it pushed out from the center, which consisted of several blocks of brick storefronts and converted Victorians. The town center was ringed by bungalows and Georgians built in the 1920s, '30s, and '40s; those were surrounded by Colonials and ranches built during the suburban sprawl of the 1950s and '60s—the mass exodus of families in lines of Oldsmobiles and Fords and Chevys gliding along the newly paved highway stretching out from the smoky, smelly city into the great green promise of space and air and a garden.

All up and down this new highway, cow paths became sidewalks, dirt roads turned asphalt, and Kentucky bluegrass swarmed the cornfields. One-room schoolhouses received twenty-room additions. Gas stations popped up on every corner to accommodate the cars that now competed for the right-of-way with the horses still put to work in the remaining fields. The suburbs were an earthly quilt of old corn acreage and new quarter-acre house plats that promised a quieter, richer life.

And dotted throughout all these plats and sidewalks were the original nineteenth-century farmhouses standing like lighthouses, remainders of a previous time.

John carried his wife across the yard toward their new home, or he would have, had he been alive. Michael was sure of it, for he'd seen his father do it before, when it rained for three days and a big pool formed outside their farmhouse door.

Here a cement walkway led to the front door, winding over the worn lawn dotted with small mirrors of brown water from a recent rain. Anne trudged along it as she carried a large suitcase toward the house, elbows out and hands up toward her belly. She slipped for a moment and lost the suitcase to the sludgy grass. She did not want to be here, but she laughed despite herself. There was a point, she always said, when laughing was all you could do.

Michael waited on the curb beside the truck's rear bumper, looking up at the house. It was unimpressive, nothing like the white clapboard farmhouse he was born in. This was small and brown and looked beaten under the two giant silver maples flanking it. The trees looked older than the house; Michael imagined they were remnants from an earlier home, perhaps a farmhouse like his. The August air was warm and tangible, gritty with exhaust and dust from the thousand homes nearby. Michael was boxed in among boxes.

A pack of boys came down the middle of the street, laughing and growling in their prepubescent conceit. As they passed, one boy noticed Michael watching them and left the pack. He stood in front of Michael a moment, then shoved him. The others laughed as Michael landed on his rump in the wet grass of the boulevard, but he had been a temporary distraction. None of the boys looked back as they continued down the street.

Michael stood and wiped his hands on the new jeans his mother made him wear for the long drive down from Minnesota. As he wiped, he looked up and caught a girl staring at him from a window across the street. Embarrassed, he smiled, but she turned around and walked back into the dark of her house.

"Alright, Michael, your turn," he imagined his father saying as he reached down to lift him up. He came unexpectedly, in small moments.

Michael knew he'd have waved him away. "I don't need your help."

Michael grabbed a suitcase handle with two hands, like his mother, and ambled toward the front door, the suitcase knocking against his knees with every step. He imagined his father's large feet in front of him and tried to place his own inside the footprint left behind. How often he had walked behind his father on paths through woods and fields, places he could see now, fresh and clear as a northern lake.

After changing into shorts and putting his clothes away in the closet, Michael took his old patchwork quilt out of a large black trash bag and laid it on the twin bed, but it was all wrong. His books and lamp and baseball cards did not belong here, either. These things were not where they were supposed to be. Nothing was. As he stood staring at this unfamiliar room with thin olive-green carpeting, he heard the sound of dishes scraping together as his mother unpacked in the kitchen, not his kitchen.

He needed to breathe. He decided to take a walk around the block to get an idea of where he was. They didn't have sidewalks where he came from—a simple thing, but he noticed. He thought it made everything seem very organized. He wondered what would happen if he walked on the street, but he stayed on the sidewalk. Basketball hoops held court above several driveways, but no one was playing. The schoolyard at the end of his street was empty save a chain-link backstop and some squirrels.

He didn't even see the girl in the window across the street again, not when he walked out, not when he returned. His mother stood planting pink geraniums in the boxes under the windows on either side of the brown front door. Michael sat on the front stoop and put his chin in his hands.

"You'll just have to learn what children do here," she said. "Why don't you go back out? Walk a few blocks farther."

At the school at the end of his street, Michael turned left on the sidewalk instead of turning right to walk around the block again. He saw rows of houses with red brick and white siding, bikes on lawns, rainbow towels laid out as if someone had been sunbathing. A few kids rode by, and Michael followed their direction.

He tried to discern each dip of the sidewalk, each curve of the land beneath the lawns. He wondered whether he was walking on an old cornfield or through an old hog shed. And even before that, what animals roamed here. Was there a creek beneath the street, filled in long ago, where coyotes used to drink? Had Indians camped here, a hunter ever landed a deer whose blood leaked into the earth at his feet? This was a game he used to play with his parents whenever they went to Minneapolis, a city of concrete surrounded by prairie. At the horse races on the edge of the city, Michael and his parents, perched high in the grandstand, would look out over the track to the rising steel buildings beyond and re-imagine the old world. Even on their own farm, Michael's father pointed out that it was once covered in forest and dominated by wolves, bobcats, and bears. Now their farm held a new family.

The ache in Michael's body, always present lately, pulsed harder. It was as if he had two knotted balls, one in his throat, one in his stomach, throbbing together, beating away the oxygen. At a corner, he sat down on the curb to catch his breath. As he waited, Michael thought back to the wolves, to the first time his father let him come along to sit with him in the woods and watch. It was the only time, late last winter. The day they found the grandmother wolf caught in a trap. The day before his father died. Before.

For as long as Michael could remember, his father had risen early most Sundays and walked off alone into the woods. He never brought his gun, or even a book. These moments were not for hunting or distraction, he said. They were not a chore or a responsibility. These moments were for him. He would sit and wait and watch. There was one pack in the area, and he knew each of them individually. He knew where they liked to hunt, where they often played. In the spring, he knew in which of several pack dens the mother—usually only one—birthed her pups. He'd sit for hours, said you could learn a lot by watching wolves. At the end he was always satisfied, even if the wolves didn't appear. The answer is always in nature, he said.

"Not much longer," said John.

They'd left the grandmother wolf an hour ago, and Michael hadn't stopped thinking about her. He wondered whether they should have taken her, put her on a sled and brought her back to her den. But he trusted his father, knew he would have done what was best.

They came to a tiny clearing where the woods thinned. John placed pine boughs on the ground to cover the cold earth and snow, then sat, leaning against the stump of a broken tree. Michael sat next to him and followed his gaze across a small field dotted with trees to a low hill beyond.

"If we're not too late, we'll see them come out of there," he said.

They waited in the silence that surrounded them. Michael would not have spoken even had he anything to say, for he recognized he was a guest at his father's clearing. Sitting nestled next to him, Michael was warm. He looked at his father, his brown hair peeking out from under his knit hat at the ears, his large features big enough for a land like Minnesota. Michael couldn't picture him anywhere else.

Calmed, Michael stood up from the curb. He turned the corner and suddenly came upon a large field with several backstops in the distance. But again, no children. He walked across the field, wiping sweat from his forehead with the back of his hand. The humidity, too, reminded him of home, and the grass he walked on emanated moisture like the farm fields. A parking lot in the distance was full of cars. Promising, though only a few people played tennis on the other side of the lot. Up the hill to his right was a building. A movie theater? A library? Michael walked up the hill and saw and heard it at the same time: a swimming pool, a large rectangle of aquamarine glaring in the sun, holding dozens of people splashing, dripping, and gliding. He had never seen a pool before, had only heard of them. Back home everyone swam at the lake or in the creeks cutting through fields.

He stood at the chain-link fence surrounding the pool and watched. Several older girls lay on their towels, greasy with oil, smoking cigarettes. A group of young boys and girls sat in a clump on a wooden deck near a concession stand, eating red licorice ropes and pretzel rods. Mothers sat in low chairs, bouncing babies in white sun hats on their laps. Boys ran along the cement and landed like cannonballs in the water, soaking those sitting at the edge of the pool. Three diving boards lined the far end, and children waited their turn, the longest line snaking away from the high dive. He smelled coconut and sugar and the mildew of wet towels.

Michael looked down at his shorts. They would do for swimming. He didn't have a towel, but the air was so hot he wouldn't need one. He walked around the fence to the building entrance, where a girl sat in a little cubicle reading a magazine. When she saw Michael, she closed the magazine and clasped her hands in front of her.

"May I help you?" she asked crisply, with hard edges.

"I'd like to go in," he said.

"Do you have a pass?"

"No."

"Are you a resident?"

"Of?"

She cocked her head. "Of Ackerman."

"Yes," said Michael.

"Three dollars."

"Oh. I don't have three dollars."

The girl raised her eyebrows. "Well, then you can't go in."

"How do I get a pass?" he asked.

She pointed to another door. "Through there. But if you don't have three dollars, then you probably don't have seventy-five, either."

"It's seventy-five dollars to get a pass?"

"For the whole season. Though the season's almost over, so maybe they'll give it to you cheaper."

Michael walked through the door, not to get a pass—he wouldn't think of asking his mother to spend the money—but to ask whether, as a new resident unfamiliar with pools, he might try a swim to see if he liked it enough to pay three dollars every time. He was not normally so bold; the clean, clear water simply looked too inviting. But the man behind the desk suggested he just pay the three dollars like everyone else. Michael walked back home.

"I don't know why it's so hard to go swimming here," he told his mother, still planting flowers.

"They need a way to pay for the pool," she said. "Go take the money out of my purse."

But now that Michael was home, he felt timid. He didn't want to walk into the pool alone, sit by himself, swim by himself.

"I'll just go tomorrow," he told his mother.

He walked to the backyard, to the one interesting thing about the house: a brown and tan shed fashioned like a mini-barn. The owners kept a lawn mower in it, a stool, and a workbench with several tools. They told Michael's mother they would take ten dollars off the monthly rent if she or Michael mowed the lawn and shoveled the snow, which she accepted. It was a push mower, not a riding one like Michael was used to, but he would be glad to have something to do. He missed the rhythm and function of farm life. Pike, the smell of a cow, the familiar patch of grass worn from walking between the garage and barn. So many things. He thought about them all as he sat on a stool in the cool dark of the shed.

"Give it time. Before you pass judgment," Anne said one night after dinner, as Michael lay on the floor with a crossword puzzle and she sat on the couch reading. "School starts soon. You'll find plenty of friends then."

She watched her son study the crossword with his tongue sticking partly out of his mouth, pencil grasped between smudged fingers.

Anne was an older parent. Most women her age were on their third child by the time she and John brought Michael home from the agency when she was thirty years old. They had tried and tried to have a baby, and after many years of wishing, hoping, excitement, crying, and resolve, they adopted. John told Anne later he had thought there was a possibility he would not love it as much as his own, and so he had planned to react how he knew he should at the sight of his new son, this child from someone else thrust into his arms. As he and Anne ascended the stairs at the agency, he readied himself to tear up at the sight of the baby, and it pained him to think that his wife might know he was trying too hard.

There was no need. A nurse brought the sleeping baby over to the couple and placed him into Anne's arms. John looked at the face in repose and thought, *Mine.*

He itched for a turn to hold his son, and when he was finally cradling the small head and warm body, he did cry. The connections of life, the web of the universe, all the worn truisms about the broad and vast scope of knowledge and time and matter were evident, and he felt the gravity in his heart.

At home later that day, John, feeling quite clannish, remembered that a drawing of the family crest lay in a drawer somewhere and dug it out. On the crest was written, *Sage Avec Esperance.* Wisdom with hope. He hung the crest above little Michael's crib, and as he looked at it, he saw clearly the parts of his own father he would reject. He would not drink at home. He would attend all school events. He would never call his son a sissy. He would play catch whenever, if ever, his son wanted. It hadn't been until John was sixteen that he found out his own father, who wrote with his right hand, threw a baseball with his left.

There had been so much to do since John's death, so many things to tick off lists, Anne had been able to keep the pain, the destructive pain, at bay, though she worried she could not accomplish it all with an easy grace so that Michael's life would be uninterrupted. Michael was quiet, she often thought, like the woods around their home. Their old home. She would need to pay attention. He'd been raised in the embrace of a small community where quiet didn't matter. He had been born into his friends.

That night, Anne woke early again, at four thirty in the morning. She stood in her nightgown and gazed out the window at the black night. Just as still, she told herself, as the farm. She did not hear Michael in the next room and was glad for that. She would not peek her head in to check. Keep him sleeping, keep him sleeping. She was sure he was.

At five o'clock she saw several lights blink on in other houses, as they had each morning since they moved in a few days ago. She imagined wives rolling toward their husbands for a hug before rising, as she'd once done, and she grew lonesome—the lights a reminder that she was alone, in her room and in her neighborhood, a farmer's wife standing solitary in a sea of houses.

These women, whom she'd come to know only through the window, would soon leave their homes for the train station, headed to Chicago. They'd walk out their doors in nylons and gym shoes, a briefcase in one hand and high heels in the other. Those with babies lugged them into station wagons, driving off to daycares, she supposed. It was a life she didn't know. She thought of her own pickup truck in the driveway.

The other day, Anne read an article about a new brand of woman who could "have it all." She wondered whether that was possible. For her, it had been an easy choice. She loved farm life. She loved mothering. She'd pursued higher education because she also loved knowledge. She felt at peace with her choice. The delicate moments of childhood—the moment when Michael first put two words together ("Hi Mama") or the moment when he first threw his head back in laughter, the first time, ever, this little human did that— those moments were gone in an instant, and they seemed even to her to be moments that were almost missed.

Anne considered herself lucky to have been able to stay home with Michael for this long. Her brother had agreed to let her off at three thirty every afternoon instead of five so she could be home for Michael after school. She would be there when he walked through the door as she always had been. She would sit with him over a snack and listen about his day, watch his brow for signs of trouble. Answer his questions, soothe his concerns. This was her plan.

Anne lay back down on top of the covers and dozed. At seven, someone knocked on the front door. She sat up and threw on her robe. As she passed Michael's room, she heard a page turn. *He must be reading,* she thought, *and she hoped he would come out so she could see his little face.*

When Anne opened the door, a large wicker basket filled with blueberry muffins moved toward her.

"Oh my," she said, grabbing the basket because there was nothing else to do.

"Morning!" said a voice behind the basket, and Anne stepped back to allow a better view. "I hope I'm not too early." Anne saw a heavy woman with gray hair, rolled and styled, standing on her front step. Her short-sleeved floral silk blouse was weighted down in the center by several gold necklaces lying on her large breast. Wrinkled, suede-soft arms extended to clasp hands on her belly.

"No," said Anne, touching her robe. "Excuse my appearance."

The woman waved her away. "I'm early, I know. Can't help myself. I baked the muffins; I didn't want to sit around waiting to bring them."

Anne opened the door wider. "Please come in, Miss . . . ?"

"Wilderhausen. Mrs. Aggie Wilderhausen."

Anne held out her hand. "Anne Nygaard."

Mrs. Wilderhausen raised an eyebrow. "Nygaard? What's that—Dutch?"

"Norwegian."

Mrs. Wilderhausen nodded. "Ah, yes. I'd heard you were from Minnesota. MinnEeeSohTah."

Anne grinned. "Hopefully I don't sound like that."

Mrs. Wilderhausen looked around the room. "Well, I see you've settled in. It's taken me too long to get over." She turned to Anne. "My health isn't what it once was, you know."

"I'm sorry to hear that."

"Me too. I suppose it's just what happens. You're born, you grow, you die. Like my peonies." Mrs. Wilderhausen sighed and shook her head.

Anne held up the basket. "Would you like some coffee and muffins?"

Mrs. Wilderhausen sat at the kitchen table as Anne scooped ground coffee out of a tin.

"I've seen your boy around, but I haven't seen a man."

Anne poured a pot of water into the coffeemaker. Mrs. Wilderhausen was waiting, quiet behind her. *Let her ask*, thought Anne.

"You work then, I suppose," said Mrs. Wilderhausen.

Anne sealed the plastic lid on the coffee can and turned around. "I'll be starting at Murphy's Tavern. My brother is the owner."

Mrs. Wilderhausen nodded. "Good burgers. Deplorable Cobb salad." She fingered her necklaces. "My daughter works. Wakes up early to get herself ready, make lunches, and wake the kids. Then off to daycare." She whisked her arms through the air.

Michael appeared in the doorway in his pajamas and bare feet, eyeing Mrs. Wilderhausen.

"Ah! Speak of the devil," she said.

He looked to his mother. "Michael," said Anne, "this is our neighbor, Mrs. Wilderhausen."

"Happy to meet you," said Mrs. Wilderhausen. "Your mother tells me you're the man of the house."

Michael watched her but said nothing. Mrs. Wilderhausen waited, then looked to Anne and back at the boy. "Shy, are we?"

"Michael just woke up," said Anne, as she set a cup of coffee in front of her new neighbor. Then she went over to Michael and placed an arm around his shoulder.

"Yes, yes," said Mrs. Wilderhausen. "And he walks out to find a stranger in his kitchen. You don't need to tell me twice. I'm early, I know. You're still in your robe, after all. What time is it? 7:30? Well. That's early, I suppose." She shrugged and sipped her coffee.

Anne smiled. "It was nice of you to bring the muffins."

Mrs. Wilderhausen smiled with her upper lip, the way she did when confused. That had sounded like a hint for her to take her leave, but she'd just now swallowed her first drink of coffee. She grabbed her cup back from the table. "How old are you, Michael?"

"Nine."

"Nine! That's young to be man of the house."

"He's not the man of the house," said Anne. "Just a boy. My boy."

Mrs. Wilderhausen motioned to the chairs. "Sit, sit. Don't let me keep you from eating your breakfast. I put real blueberries in the muffins, they'll turn your lips blue."

Anne rubbed Michael's back as she led him toward the table. "How long have you lived in the neighborhood?" she asked, reaching to pull plates from the cupboard.

"Gosh, forever. Since the homes were new. Raised three kids here. Well, I told you about the one. And two boys."

"How nice." Anne smiled as she sat and passed the plates.

"Mr. Wilderhausen works in insurance. Hates it. Just hates it. He'll retire soon. Good God, have I been lucky. Never had to work a day in my life. Well, unless you count the children, which certainly was work. I don't need to tell you." She winked at Anne and grabbed a muffin. "Yes, lucky as stars. Good thing, too. My boys needed me when they reached an age. Oh, it was about thirteen. Lord knows they'd be in jail if they didn't have me at home." Mrs. Wilderhausen took a large bite out of the muffin and chewed, looking at Anne. "Shame you have to work," she said.

Anne only nodded.

Mrs. Wilderhausen wiped her lips with her thumb. "Talkative bunch, you are," she said, with a raised eyebrow.

"We say what's necessary."

"Right. Well then," said Mrs. Wilderhausen, brushing her fingers over her plate. "I'll be off." She grabbed the basket of muffins and walked out. Anne smiled at Michael next to her and put her forehead to his. But she thought of windows, and others' lights blinking on in the dark.

Four

August 18, 1983

Dear Rose,

I'm here. Ackerman seems lovely—I drove by several blocks of quaint shops and restaurants on my way in. My apartment is above a drug store that I have to walk through to get to the door that leads up to my apartment. The store has one of those old-fashioned counters. A bunch of men were standing around smoking and drinking coffee just now. This must be a gathering place. Who knows, maybe I'll join the crowd and take up smoking. You'd disapprove, but then, you are always setting a good example.

Right outside the drugstore door is a giant honey locust. I see the leaves through my window now and am reminded of our backyard.

Love,
Julia

The letter was almost purely informational, but it would have to do. Julia did not have the energy for what Rose deserved. She would write that letter when she was settled.

She looked around her apartment, a big white square with a kitchen, and a bedroom off that. Her clothes were already hung in the closet, but everything else sat in boxes. She'd packed a futon, books, a small television, and other knickknacks that fit in her car. She didn't have time for anything else. Or rather, she didn't want to take anything more from Rose, to leave with more than she already was.

A bed was on its way, but she still needed chairs, a couch, a dresser. She was glad, actually, to have something to do. There was a week until school started, and though she found immediate comfort in the white anonymity of her apartment, the starkness also made it quite easy to see what wasn't there.

She left, hoping to glide through the drugstore unnoticed. But she made eye contact with the man behind the counter, and he smiled, so she offered a tight-lipped grin. She had no desire to make friends.

Julia walked three blocks to a used-furniture store she remembered seeing when she arrived in town and had remarkable success; her apartment was outfitted in an hour. The young woman behind the counter barely looked at her as she rang up Julia's items and scheduled the delivery. As she walked home, past a Baskin-Robbins, a clothing boutique, a used-books shop, faceless people flew past. No one noticed her, and she reveled in the freedom, breathing in the summer breeze as she pushed her blonde hair behind her ears. She could be anyone.

She folded her arms across her middle, her purse hanging from her forearm and swaying with her skirt. Smiling despite herself, she looked down to hide it so passersby wouldn't think she was crazy. On she walked, people parting around her. When she looked up, she stood on a corner facing a newspaper vending machine and a headline that read, "AIDS 4-H Club: homosexuals, hemophiliacs, heroin addicts, and Haitians."

She stopped, and people continued to brush by her, rudely knocking her shoulder, her hip, her purse. Their eyes burned her skin, and the newspaper screamed inside her head. After a frozen moment, she stepped away from the vending machine and bumped into a stroller. The woman pushing it eyed her, and Julia felt her anonymity was gone.

The jewelry dish broke when she flung it from the box onto the floor. Newspaper flew through the air, fast at first before floating down. A ring box without a ring, a notebook, pencils bound by a rubber band, her third grade diary with a girl picking flowers on the front, all of these tossed as Julia searched box after box. Her apartment was too small and the walls nagged her. She realized she'd forgotten to buy paintings.

When she found the picture of Rose, she held it up and was disappointed to find it provided less comfort than she thought it would. Compared to the real Rose, it was flat, featureless. Nothing of the rounded, dimpled cheeks that made Rose always look happy. Nothing of the girlish corkscrew curls that shined brown like her mother's antique brass doorknobs. But Julia was determined, so she looked and looked and thought about the two of them as girls until the tears dropped.

There had been a time when Julia would have done anything for Rose—all of the time since they were five up until recently, in fact. What happened recently changed everything. Julia had been sure the obstacles did not matter, but she had been wrong, not in the way those are who have never known true obstacles, but in a testament to her ability to see all things as fine. Everything's fine.

Where once Julia had seen Rose as a sort of savior from her mother's stricture, now she was a reminder that Julia was not normal. Not fine.

They had been normal once.

They came together over a little black girl named Tabitha on the first day of kindergarten. As she skipped rope, her braided pigtails flying, several boys threw stones at the little girl's feet, trying to make her fall. She ignored them and continued jumping. She sang a playground song, even when one of the pebbles hit her cheek. But Rose came running from one side of the playground and Julia from the other.

"Stop it!" yelled Rose. Julia stood over the stones, blocking the boys. She knew throwing stones at a little girl was not polite.

"Whatever," said one of the boys, and they ran off.

Back inside, Rose saved a seat for Julia at snack time, and from then on they were best friends—"kindred spirits," said Rose, all dimples and chestnut curls. Tabitha was in another class, but Julia and Rose played with her every recess. One day, Julia brought Rose and Tabitha home with her.

Julia's mother was raised in rural Kansas but educated at a prestigious women's school in the East, and so she prided herself on her worldly views. But old notions die hard, especially when they're not recognized as being old.

Julia's mother smiled at Tabitha, laid out lemonade and cookies, and left them to their play.

But once the cookies were gone and the girls had spent an hour coloring and Tabitha and Rose had gone home, Mrs. Parnell said, "Tabitha is no longer welcome here."

"Why, Mama?"

Julia's mother kneeled down to her. "Because she's colored, Julia. Clean, but a nigger nonetheless. Please tell Rose not to bring her here anymore. I'm surprised she thought it was appropriate in the first place, without even asking."

Julia didn't tell her mother that it had been her idea.

At recess the next day, Julia found herself staring at the white tips of Tabitha's nails. She looked at her neck and ears and her shining black hair. She was sad her mother disapproved, for Tabitha was the smartest girl in kindergarten, even in math. She always wore bows at the ends of her braided pigtails and dresses with puffed sleeves. But her mother was clear, and though Julia had a little ball of feeling in the center of her chest, she believed her when she said it was wrong to play with her.

When she told Rose that her mother forbade having Tabitha over, Rose just cocked her head and said, "Huh," as if she had figured something out. Julia didn't know what it was, but Rose was always doing that. Then Rose shrugged her shoulders and said, "We'll play at my house."

But Julia's mother forbade her from that, too, if Tabitha was there. Julia cried, but her mother was firm. She told Rose the next day at school, and Rose cocked her head again, and then a moment later grabbed Julia's hand and pulled her onto the playground, leaving Tabitha to skip rope alone. Rose had made her choice because it had to be made.

From then on, they were inseparable. They wrote notes to each other in class, even mailed letters back and forth though they saw each other every day. "It's more meaningful," said Rose. As they grew, their bond intensified behind closed doors of bedrooms with posters tacked on the wall and record albums on the stereo. It was innocent enough, but Julia's mother always cracked the door open a bit. She hadn't forgiven Rose for bringing Tabitha over, and she told Julia that she and Rose were closer than any two girls needed to be.

"And I don't like the way she looks at me," said Julia's mother one day, pausing from her work polishing the silverware. "As if she knows something about me I don't know."

"Oh, Mama," said Julia. She sat on a dining room chair, carefully placing a fork back in its place in the box. "She's just interested in people."

"No girl has any business looking at an adult that way. My father would have slapped that look right off me."

By this age, Julia knew her grandfather *never* would have done that, for it would have been quite unseemly, and she said as much.

"Not in front of anyone, maybe," her mother responded.

Julia was voted "Most Likable" by her senior class—"My word!" said her mother—and graduated with honors. When she was accepted into a small liberal arts college on the Illinois shores of Lake Michigan, Rose followed. They were roommates, but because of her mother's protests that Julia should branch out and make new friends, Julia kept it a secret and asked Rose to stay with a friend every time her parents visited.

"Your mother needs to chill," said Rose.

"If the scotch and cigarettes haven't done it yet, nothing will," said Julia. "Of course, it's always precisely one scotch and one cigarette at precisely five o'clock."

When Julia and Rose decided to take a trip together for spring break sophomore year, Julia's mother had had enough.

"Don't you have any other friends?" she asked over the phone. "It's not appropriate, you spending so much time with her like you do. One might think you two were dating, for heaven's sake." She let out a nervous laugh.

"Rose is my best friend, Mother. We've been best friends since kindergarten."

"She's keeping you from people. She's possessive."

"She is not. I have other friends." Julia twirled the phone cord around her finger. "Please, Mother. Stop."

But Julia's mother did not stop. She informed Julia over the phone the following week that she and her father could no longer afford to pay her private school tuition. Julia would have to drop out and enroll at the University of Kansas to finish her education degree. In a small act of defiance, Julia applied to and was accepted at the University of Iowa instead. Her mother consented, thinking, "Anywhere but with Rose."

The separation did nothing to weaken the friendship, though, and their habit of correspondence continued more intensely. "Kindred spirits are always kindred spirits," said Rose. "It can't be helped."

Julia stayed hidden in her stale white apartment for two straight days, alternating between unpacking and watching summer reruns. She saw people walk by on the sidewalk below, watched the slivered leaves of the honey locust rattle in the breeze an arms-length away from her window. When the furniture was delivered, she wasn't prepared, so the men placed the pieces wherever there was room. After they left, Julia sat on her hands on her new old blue couch, which stretched diagonally across the room. Her dresser, a table, chairs, and bookshelves rose up around her.

She felt comfortably small and reminded herself that she was still free—still gone from Iowa. Still where no one really knew her. Rising, she grabbed her purse. She would just order something to drink, perhaps some tea. A strip of light at the bottom of the stairs guided her, and when she opened the door, she met the smell of smoke, chocolate, Band-aids, and Kotex. It was familiar to her, the smell of every drug store she'd ever been in. A long gray Formica counter lined with shiny metal stools with black cushioned seats was on her right; perpendicular to that, neck-high rows of shelves filled the store, each ending a few feet from the glass storefront. She gave a slight nod to the men gathered at the far end of the counter, and they nodded back. Exhaling, she sat down with her purse in her lap. She'd never loved tea but had been raised drinking it. Her mother thought coffee was not as dignified.

A man about her age came over, wiping the counter as he said, "What can I get you?"

"What do you have?" she asked, glad to get right to the point without chitchat.

"We keep it simple. Coffee, tea, or hot chocolate. Once in a while I'll have a box of stale donuts or something else from the shelves." He extended his hand. "I'm Andy."

"Oh." She grabbed it. "Julia."

"You live upstairs."

"Yes."

"What brings you here?"

Julia pushed her hair behind her ear. "I'll be teaching fourth grade at the elementary school."

"Ah, one of those, are you?"

"Those?"

"Saints. It takes one to teach children, I think."

Julia blushed and placed her elbows on the counter. "No children?"

"God, no. Too immature for that. Plus, I'm here every waking hour."

"Are you the owner?" This seemed easy, talking with Andy.

"Me? No, but I might as well be."

Julia glanced toward the men at the other end of the bar. "They seem to be here a lot."

"Almost every day. If it's before three, they drink coffee. If it's after, they order coffee but add the liquor they bring with them." Andy shrugged. "I pretend I don't know. Sometimes they even bring in those red plastic cups. Don't know who they think they're fooling."

"Why don't they just go to a bar?" asked Julia. "There's one around the corner."

Andy leaned on the counter. "Well, that wouldn't be respectable, going to a bar every day. Plus, their wives would catch wind. So they come here."

"Are they a good bunch?"

"For the most part. I have some stories."

Julia watched them, several older men, probably retired. They were portly and balding, jovial, familiar. Among them were a couple of younger, middle-aged men, and Julia imagined they probably worked with their hands, construction maybe.

Andy leaned closer. "I probably know a lot more than they think I do. Liquor has a way of making people think they're whispering when really their voices could wake the dead."

Julia giggled, something she had not done for some time.

Andy straightened. "So what can I get you?"

"Tea, please." She opened her purse to find her wallet.

"We don't get a lot of tea drinkers, here," he said. "Let me see if I can find the hot water pot."

Then Julia was embarrassed. She closed her purse and sat on the stool with her hands in her lap. She could feel the glimpses from the men at the other end of the counter, wondering who she was and what she was doing here. She focused on the wall behind the counter, lined with a coffee machine, cups, cigarette racks, small stacks of scattered papers. A picture of Clint Eastwood hung above the coffee. The whole wall was framed by a string of colored Christmas lights, turned off. Julia vaguely wondered if they'd been there since last Christmas or if they were an intentional part of the decorating. She tried not to feel the men staring.

By the time Andy returned, Julia was too uncomfortable to drink. When he set down her teacup and hot water, she laid a couple of dollars on the counter and excused herself, telling him she forgot about an important phone call she needed to make.

August 25, 1983

Dear Rose,

It is so hot today I put the air conditioning unit on high, and you know how I hate air conditioning. It's giving me a headache, but it's better than sitting here in my own sweat.

Tomorrow is the first day of school. I could recite my lesson plan in my sleep, though nothing is written down. I wish you were here to chastise me for it.

Love,

Julia

Julia sealed the envelope and lay on the couch, resting her cheek against her palm. She knew the letter would make Rose mad. It wasn't fair, what Julia was doing, but it was what she knew. If she'd learned anything from her mother, it was how to deal. Julia could weather anything. There was no way to reconcile the feelings in her head and heart, and so she was determined to wait it all out. To just wait, and something would happen. Time heals all wounds, she reminded herself. But she doubted it. Time changes all wounds, allows a thicker skin to grow over. But heals? No.

When Julia graduated college last May, she persuaded Rose to come to central Iowa where she'd found a job teaching elementary school. It was out of love—it could only have been love—that Rose moved to a rural town of four thousand to start her career in journalism. Naturally, they shared an apartment. Rose often joked that Julia was like a wife, but Julia only smiled, and Rose knew she was not ready to have that conversation.

The apartment was on the second story of the yellow clapboard home of an elderly, chain-smoking widow named Jane who wore tight dungarees and red plaid shirts. She was friendly but hard in the way that Julia remembered the folks in Kansas were, those who came into town from their farms to go to the movies or sell grain. She always had the feeling they could handle anything, had handled everything. She liked being around them because she felt safe, as if nothing in the world would harm them or their town. Not with people like them around. People like Jane.

Rose and Julia had a kitchenette in their apartment, but the very first afternoon, Jane told them breakfast was at seven, so that's when they left their apartment to eat with Jane at her table. Sometimes they brought muffins, sometimes they just came down early to help. A friendship formed; it was easy with someone like Jane, who never said anything she didn't mean and assumed they did the same.

It was Jane who found Rose a job at the newspaper. The editor had been a poker friend of Jane's husband and had always, thought Jane, had a crush on her. It was also Jane who picked a vaseful of white peonies for Rose the morning of her first day.

"They were going to die anyway," she said, snapping off a brown leaf from the bunch.

Julia later learned that one Sunday morning in early June, Rose went downstairs to work on the crossword with Jane, as she often did. Just after Jane had solved eight letters for "an illicit lover," and was penciling in the letters, she looked over her bifocals and asked, "Are you and Julia together?"

Rose didn't pretend she did not understand. "No."

Jane nodded and pursed her lips, went back to the crossword. "Wouldn't be any of my business if you were," she said. "Wouldn't be anybody's business."

After a moment, Rose put down her pencil. "May I ask you something?"

"Shoot."

Rose paused, formulating the words in her head while Jane lit a cigarette. "I'm sort of—stuck. I'd like to move forward, but there's just this wall. I don't want to still be at this wall ten years from now."

"What is your question?"

"How do I get unstuck?"

Jane nodded. "Where do you want to be?"

"Living the life I think I was meant to live."

"I see," said Jane, exhaling cigarette smoke. "Why do you think I can help?"

"I've never talked about it before. What you said just now were the first words anyone has ever said to me about this. Directly, anyway."

"Well," said Jane. "I've always found that things that seem too big in one's head are much more manageable once they're said out loud. You might try talking with her."

Rose laughed. "I know. It sounds so simple."

"But it's not. No one'd claim it was. Still, it's there to do."

It was several days before Julia heard the words. Rose said them quickly, in no context, for they were just walking down the street on their way to a movie. Julia was saying something about wishing she'd remembered to bring a sweater because the theater would probably be cold, and Rose replied, "I love you."

A sound like a laugh came out of Julia. She glanced sideways at Rose but said nothing. Fear and anxiety flooded into her and cemented, blocking first thought and then feeling.

"I know you love me, too," said Rose. "It's not like either of us want to make a big deal about it, but still, it should be said. We need to move out of this middle ground where we know but don't know; where we live but don't live. We want to spend all our time with each other, we've never had real boyfriends, and we never plan to. So let's just admit what we are and get on with it."

As Rose spoke, the fear inside Julia cracked just a bit. Pieces floated up and off her. Not many, but enough. She let Rose take her hand, let herself be led down the sidewalk, and after several moments said, "Okay."

That night, Rose kissed her as she sat reading on the couch, and Julia realized she'd fooled herself into thinking that part of a relationship with Rose wouldn't have to be acknowledged. She wanted to kiss Rose, ached to kiss her, but giggles of anxiety kept erupting from her belly. This was absurd, the thought of her kissing Rose, and she couldn't help but imagine everyone's reaction—her parents, their high school friends, her former professors. *My goodness, people will be surprised*, she thought. And, she feared, disgusted. Their faces would not leave her mind.

"I'm sorry, I'm sorry," she said, when Rose grew frustrated. "I don't know what's wrong with me."

"Nothing's wrong with you," said Rose, exhaling and moving away to the other side of the couch. "It'll take time."

The next day, Julia cleaned the apartment, light and happy. Afternoon sun streamed through the windows, highlighting the dust she swept off of tables. She relished this feeling of summer freedom, perhaps enhanced now that she and Rose had said the unspoken. She heard a knock.

She opened the door to find Rose with a bouquet of flowers.

"What are you doing?" Julia asked. Her neck muscles tightened, and she glanced down the hall though she knew hers was the only apartment on the floor.

Rose beamed, her dimples deep. "I'm here to ask you on a date."

"You didn't need to knock."

"I've seen you around town, and I understand you'll be teaching at the elementary school. I thought to myself, This is the type of woman I want to date."

Julia inhaled, embarrassed. She knew she was supposed to laugh and be touched, so she said, "You're a goof," but she thought of her mother's parties, when her mother would ask each attendee to sit in a folding chair placed in a circle in the living room and name her favorite book or casserole dish. If men were present, she asked them to name their favorite drink. Julia always felt awkward—took on the awkwardness—for the people in the living room as she sat listening on the stairs. The ickiness would fill her up to gagging. But once that part was over, she could feel the relief that flooded into the room and caused people to begin chatting as they otherwise might not have had they not just been forced to do something so unnatural.

Rose continued. "Since we've already known each other for, like, twenty years, I decided we'll just have to forget that little fact and start over. As far as I can tell, this is how people begin dating."

Julia felt the relief flood in, just a little. "You know I hate carnations."

"No, I didn't know that. We've only just met."

Julia grabbed Rose's elbow and pulled her inside. "Yes, I'll go on a date with you." She took the flowers and placed them on a table, then threw her arms around Rose's neck because she knew it was what she should do, but also because it started to feel right.

"You're playing me." She nudged Rose's nose with her own.

Then.

And then it was like Julia always pictured, ever since she read her first love story and saw for the first time a couple holding hands—it was an old couple, their spotted knuckles bent in around each other's as they ambled side by side, and even at her young age, Julia wondered at wanting to hold someone's hand for that long; she knew it was odd, uncommon, to be that old doing something as young and fleeting as holding hands.

This was like that. New, yet familiar.

They were awkward, trembling fingers and quivering lips. Julia covered herself with the sheet at first, but she let Rose in. She lay in Rose's arms and closed her eyes and forgot her mother or their friends back home. She forgot even herself.

That summer was gilded with a haze of yellow, glowing like the light right next to a candle. Julia, not yet working, accompanied Rose on newspaper assignments to city council and school board meetings. She sat in folding chairs with her, carried her camera, recited the addresses as Rose drove. Each moment was ripe with the possibility that they might leave the room and meet in a bathroom stall, or in the stairwell, or pull over to the side of the road and go off into a group of oaks in a farmer's field.

Julia, for the first time in memory, had her own world with Rose. She was not home where people knew her, where expectations encased her like a plaster cast. She was not in college, trying to make friends, pleasing. She was in the middle of nowhere. Grown up. Free. The only soul who knew about her and Rose was Jane, and Jane treated them with such a lack of self-consciousness that even Julia forgot there might be something for her to be self-conscious about. These weeks felt like happy years, so intense was each moment, so lived in. Julia was wild. She walked around the apartment naked, like a grown hippie, took Rose in dark building corners where they were likely to get caught. One day as they sunbathed in the backyard, separated from other yards by wooden fences over which second-story windows peered, Julia untied her top and let it fall off. Rose arched an eyebrow toward her but said nothing.

"It's like you're inside me," Julia told Rose that night, as she combed Rose's wavy, wet hair. "Every cell in my body is jumping with you."

Julia started to dread the beginning of school. She put off organizing her lesson plans and purchasing supplies for the classroom. Afraid to do anything that might alter her reality, she stayed near Rose, close enough to breathe the same air and keep the rest of the world out.

In mid-July, Julia received an invitation from the mother of one of her new students, Ethan Schmidt. The hand-written note read, "We would love to have you and a guest over for lunch this Saturday at noon, to welcome you before the school year."

Julia was unsure what to do about "a guest."

"Of course I'll go with you," said Rose.

"But," said Julia, "isn't that awkward?"

"Why?"

"Because 'and guest' usually means a date."

"So I'll be your date."

"I'm not sure that . . ." Julia did not know what she was trying to say, and so she didn't finish. If Rose was bothered by Julia's hesitation, she didn't show it. She was eager to let the world in.

The two of them showed up on the Schmidts' front step that Saturday at noon. A young boy Julia presumed to be Ethan opened the door.

"Hi!" He motioned for them to come in and ran off to get his mother. Mrs. Schmidt entered the foyer wiping her hands on her apron. She looked taken aback for just a moment, and then extended her hand first to Julia and then to Rose.

"I'm so glad you could make it. Please, come in. We're having chicken pot pies and salad, hope that works for you."

"It sounds delicious," said Rose, taking off her coat. Julia followed.

During lunch, the conversation flowed easy and light-hearted. Rose and Mrs. Schmidt bonded over their disdain for current fashion—"Honestly, leg warmers? I can't take anyone who wears leg warmers seriously," said Mrs. Schmidt—and their fondness for the piano.

"I've been playing since I was ten," said Rose. "I remember my first lesson the teacher asked what I knew, and I began playing 'Chopsticks.'" She laughed. "Julia remembers. I played it over and over and over. She was happy when I finally learned 'Greensleeves.'"

"You two grew up together, then?" said Mrs. Schmidt, and Julia thought she detected a mild relief, as if that explained why Julia would bring Rose, why they lived together in a place so far from home.

When they left, Rose commented on what a nice time she'd had.

"Me, too," said Julia. "Though did you see the look on her face when she first walked in and saw you?"

"No," said Rose. "I didn't. And if she had a look, it certainly disappeared. I thought she was very nice."

"Oh, yes," said Julia. "She is. Very nice. I just thought she seemed a bit surprised."

"Maybe she was."

"It probably didn't mean anything," said Julia.

Late that afternoon, Rose brought out a blanket to the backyard and they lay in the shade reading *The Des Moines Register*. Rose had a plate of krackling before her, a cinnamon and sugar pastry from the Dutch bakery in town. For the two months they'd lived here, Rose had gone to the bakery nearly twice a week, ever since they happened upon it during one of their first walks. For some reason, this time it bothered Julia.

"You can't lay off those, can you?" she said.

Rose licked her fingers. "They should bring these to peace summits." She flipped over, lay on her back, and opened the front section of the newspaper. "Huh. The House voted to censure Crane and Studds. 'For sexual misconduct involving congressional pages.' Well, I'll be. Two white men actually got in trouble for having sex with minors. Course, one of them was gay."

Julia scanned the Home section, trying to focus on pictures of living room couches and beige curtains, when the word "Ackerman" caught her eye. She knew that place, a small town in Illinois; it was familiar to her from her college days on the shores of Lake Michigan. She looked closely at the advertisement in the lower left-hand corner of the page among a scattering of other classifieds: "Fourth Grade Teacher, Certification required, starting August."

Julia quietly tore the ad from the corner of the page and placed it in her pocket. She wasn't sure what she would do with it, only that she wanted to keep it.

One day soon after, the checkout clerk at the bakery winked at her. That was all—just a wink. A friendly gesture that deep down Julia knew held no harm. That day, instead of stopping herself, Rose had sent Julia to the bakery, and the clerk had said, "Quite a sweet tooth that Rose has, huh?" and winked at her. Julia had no idea who this clerk was or how she knew that Julia knew Rose—knew, probably, that they lived together. And Julia's bubble, already thinning at the edges, broke. And then Julia was no longer free.

Two phone interviews and two weeks later, Julia was in her car, driving down the long road away from Iowa. Away from Rose.

Five

At ten o'clock in the morning, Anne climbed the steps of Murphy's Tavern, named after the dog she and her brother had when they were little. The tavern was in a Victorian brick building on a corner in the middle of town. Her slender body pulled open the heavy wooden door, and she was greeted by the smell of last night's revelry, at once sour and smoky, moist and mildewy. Sepia-toned pictures of the building's history lined the walls: a man and woman, grim and severe, standing with a horse in front of the building in 1888, with painted letters on the large window behind them spelling, "Sparrow's Grocery"; the same man and woman standing behind a wooden counter inside the building, with baskets, bins, and sacks around them showcasing flour, sugar, "New! Log Cabin Syrup," and tobacco; Model T's and Model A's parked along the curb in front of the building, which now hosted a sign reading, "Al's"; a smiling, laughing group of men and one woman waving miniature flags around a table filled with papers, buttons, and a typewriter in the middle of the large room with a banner reading "Nixon's the One!"

She walked through the maze of square tables, their wood nicked and worn from thousands of customers, chairs upturned on top, and saw her brother standing across the room, reading a clipboard. Struck by how tall he appeared, she wondered why she hadn't noticed at the funeral. Maybe it was just here, on his own ground. His straight brown hair, the same winter brown as her own, as Michael's, fell down from his forehead as he read while he tapped a pencil against the board.

That morning, unsure how to dress, she'd put on slacks and a cotton blouse. It was just a bar, but she did not want to appear unprofessional. She noticed Kevin wore jeans.

"It's just a bar," he said and smiled. "Jeans and a Murphy's T-shirt. Nothing fancy."

She followed him down a set of stairs to the basement. Two men chopped vegetables at a large stainless steel table. The back wall was lined with inventory—bread, jars of olives, napkins. Another wall of stainless steel freezers stored meat and ice cream.

They walked past the men into an office that seemed more of a storage room. There was a desk scattered with papers surrounded by shelves of liquor bottles, stacks of accounting books, a television on top of which balanced a leaning tower of VHS tapes. Kevin walked around a high chair and opened a closet that contained stacks of navy blue shirts, jackets on hangers, boxes of paper, and a large safe.

"Here's your apron and T-shirt," said Kevin. "You can put it on in the bathroom. First one is free. If you want another, it'll be seven dollars." He threw her an apologetic smile. "Same as all the employees."

"Okay."

"You get one free meal per shift, which you can come in early for or stay late. If it's really dead, you can try to squeeze it in during."

"Okay." She followed him back up the stairs.

"You'll be with Nancy today." He pointed to a woman who had begun taking down chairs. "She's been here ten years, so she'll train you well. Put your purse there." He pointed to a cubby in the waitress station.

"Okay."

"Good luck. Let me know if you need anything. You're on till four, right?"

"Three thirty."

"Right. Come say goodbye when you go." He began to leave, then turned back. "Anne, I'm glad you're here. I know you'd rather not have to be."

Anne smiled up at him as she tied her apron behind her back. "It'll work."

As she watched him walk away, she remembered that the two of them used to like to pretend they were twins. The thought came so suddenly, in a rush, that Anne just stood there for a moment. April 20, that was their shared birthday. Gosh, she hadn't thought of that date in decades. For several years in grade school, they insisted their parents hold their parties together on that day, exactly in between their actual birthdays. When had they stopped? Anne couldn't remember. She could barely see the boy in the man her brother had become. Where once he seemed scrawny and fragile, he now appeared accomplished, almost brawny. He'd filled into himself.

He'd had a hard time growing up, never seemed to find his footing with the other kids. He had a horrible lisp well into middle school and thick glasses like every nerd on the black-and-white television shows. *What a target he'd made*, thought Anne. And yet he was relentlessly friendly; he always smiled when he was picked for a team during recess, even if they picked him last. He always laughed at truly funny jokes, even if the person who told the joke had just the day before asked him to say, in front of a circle of kids, "Sally sells seashells by the seashore," knowing that Kevin couldn't say it without lisping. Kevin never gave in and said it, but he still laughed at their other jokes. He held doors open for girls who wouldn't talk to him. On family vacations to the shores of Lake Superior, it was Kevin who led Anne to the groups of children at the beach and introduced himself and his sister. He never stopped trying to make friends. He never seemed to mind.

Anne minded. She often used up her reserves of goodwill with the other children defending her little brother. How could she not? She remembered one Halloween night, as she and her friends trick-or-treated in town, she found him sitting on a curb alone, crying. Anne already knew why—older children stole his candy every year.

But this was the first time she'd seen him cry about it. She left her friends and sat down next to him.

"Who cares," said Anne. "They're jerks."

"I know." He dragged his forearm across his nose and sniffed. "But I found Old Man Rand's prize this year. It was under the lilac bush in his backyard."

Anne's eyes widened. "You did?"

Kevin nodded. "An entire box of Bazooka gum."

And then Anne understood why Kevin cried this time. Bazooka gum was her favorite, and whenever Kevin earned a piece from his speech therapist, he brought it home for her, holding onto it so tightly that the pink rectangle was soft and warm when she put it in her mouth.

"I don't care about the gum," she said. "Here. I've been taking two pieces at each house." She opened her bag to him.

She put her arm around his shoulders as they ambled under the streetlights and then the stars toward home.

Standing in the tavern, Anne thought back to that night with a mixture of happiness and guilt. She'd never known how to carry all the love little Kevin gave her, had always thought she could have done more to make things easier on him. Kevin, lisp-free and determined, had left Minnesota at eighteen while she was in college. Murphy's wasn't his only restaurant; he had several that kept him moving, distant, gone. He'd flown in the morning of the funeral, leaving late that night. She knew she had the right to be offended, but she could never draw up that feeling from her well, could never feel anything but love toward him and her memory of him as a child. Their relationship now was what it was, a sort of formal acquaintance. And who remembered when it happened, or how.

She slipped her T-shirt on over her blouse and walked over to Nancy, a slight woman about Anne's age, though she looked several years older. The lines in her forehead and around her mouth were as thick and hard as the mascara on her eyelashes. Vertical creases extended from her lips, from years of closing them around a cigarette.

"Just follow me today, and jump in when you can," said Nancy. "Molly's on, too. Usually one would have the inside and one outside; but since you're learning, we'll all do it together."

Molly was a college student with bright pink fingernails and a gold star on her left cheekbone. Anne didn't know if it was a tattoo or a drawing. Molly had tied her Murphy's T-shirt into a knot at her hip, and her blonde bangs were ratted to the side of her forehead.

When they finished with the chairs, the three of them wiped down the tables and placed on each a six-pack stuffed with silverware, ketchup, mustard, salt, pepper, and hot sauce, as well as a candle, a plastic table tent listing the weekly specials, and four menus. When that was finished, Nancy made coffee while Molly, because it was summer, filled a huge vat with tea and several scoopfuls of ice.

Nancy checked in with the cook and wrote the soup of the day on the chalkboard at the waitress station. When Chip the bartender arrived, she would write the drink special on the board as well.

Anne followed Nancy down the steps to the back door. The sun flooded the dark stairwell as Nancy propped open the door.

Outside, the three repeated the routine. They added black plastic ashtrays and opened the large umbrella over each table—sometimes a precarious task of balancing on a chair while bent over so the umbrella could open without hitting their faces. Each umbrella displayed a different beer logo.

"Watch out if it rained the night before," said Nancy. "You'll get splashed with water when you open the umbrella."

"Rock, paper, scissors for the ketchups and mustards?" said Molly.

"We all gotta go," replied Nancy. "She don't know where anything is. We need ice, anyways."

They headed down the remaining stairs to the basement, where the prep cooks were still chopping onions. Nancy opened the ice machine and filled two large white buckets with ice while Molly dragged two bins heavy with ketchup and mustard bottles from the cooler. She tried balancing one on top of the other so she could heave both up the stairs at the same time, though she knew this never worked.

She sighed, grabbing one bin and heading for the stairs, then returning for the second. Nancy and Anne hauled the two buckets of ice upstairs and filled the outside cooler. Molly stuffed in the condiments and closed the lid.

"What time is it?" Nancy asked.

Anne looked at her watch. "Ten to eleven."

"Just enough time for a cigarette," said Molly, as she pulled a pack out of her apron and offered one to Anne.

"I don't smoke," she said.

"Neither do I," said Nancy, as she exhaled.

"This is her fifth time quitting," explained Molly. "So give us the shit on Kevin."

"Oh, there's not much to tell," said Anne. "We haven't lived near each other for many years. You probably know more than I do."

"His house is amazing," said Molly, her eyes bright. "What's it like inside?"

"I haven't been in it, actually. There's been so much to do. It's large?"

"E-normous."

"Really? All by himself?"

"Who can figure rich people," said Nancy. "He's a good manager, though. Let's us do our thing, knows when to butt in." This didn't surprise Anne. "He's only here a couple times a week," continued Nancy. "He has Chip manage other times." She flicked her cigarette and jabbed it at the air for emphasis. "Now Chip, on the other hand. Chip'll treat you like shit, like you're there to serve him, too."

Anne only smiled. She did not know what to say, felt out of place. She was sure anything she had to talk about—crops, baking, mothering—was not relevant here.

"So," said Nancy. "Why did you move?"

"My husband passed on." Anne immediately regretted her bluntness. She could see they were uncomfortable, so she changed the subject.

"What are you studying?" she asked Molly.

Molly looked at her nails. "Oh, I don't know. Right now I'm just taking my requirements. I'm thinking I might be a teacher."

"What about you?" Anne asked Nancy.

"You're looking at it, honey. Waitress for life." She laughed a little too loud, her voice harsh with smoke.

Anne was embarrassed. "I just meant to ask about you. I didn't mean . . ."

Nancy shrugged. "Nothin' doing."

"You staying after?" Molly asked Nancy, and Nancy nodded. Molly turned to Anne. "You get two free drinks after every shift."

Anne's cheeks pinked. "I don't drink."

"Everybody drinks," said Nancy.

"It would be an absolute waste," said Molly. "They're free."

"I have to be home, anyway. For my son."

Molly smiled. "Well, *that's* a good excuse. Not drinking, on the other hand . . ."

Nancy and Molly threw their cigarettes in a bucket, and Anne followed them inside. Chip was wiping down bottles behind the massive oak counter that served as the bar—the same oak counter behind which the surly grocers stood over a century ago in the photo on the wall. Red-cushioned stools lined the bar. Molly hopped on one and lit another cigarette.

"Don't get my ashtray dirty," said Chip. His square jaw clenched.

"Chill, I'll wipe it," said Molly.

Chip looked at Anne. "You the new one?"

Anne nodded.

"She's Kevin's sister," said Molly.

The front door opened, and a weathered man peeked in.

"Not yet, Joe," said Chip. "You got five minutes."

The man closed the door and sat on the front steps to wait.

Chip finished wiping a bottle of vodka and folded his arms across his chest. He chewed on a toothpick.

"Money was missing from my drawer again," he said.

"No kidding," said Molly. "How much?"

"Two."

"I don't understand how they could not figure this out," said Molly. "There are cameras everywhere." She turned to Anne. "Every morning, Chip goes to the safe to get the drawer of cash that the manager prepped for him the night before. It's supposed to contain a hundred dollars."

"Those busboys are sly," said Chip.

"C'mon. They would never."

"How would they get it if it's in a safe?" asked Anne. "Couldn't it be the night manager?"

"No way," said Chip. "Debbie's a robot. Does what she's told. Plus, she's a mom."

Anne wasn't sure that made her definitively honest, but she didn't mind the stereotype.

Chip shrugged and grabbed at his toothpick. "I'm just saying. Busboys are in and out of that office all the time grabbing bottles for me, highchairs, receipt paper . . ."

"Maybe you miscounted," said Molly. "It's only two."

"Exactly. Small enough to make me think I'm going crazy."

The old man poked his head in the front door again.

"C'mon in," said Chip, and Joe ambled toward the bar. He took off his sweat-stained baseball cap and placed it down.

"What'll it be?" asked Chip.

Joe crept onto a stool. "Light draft, please."

"Sure thing."

The first table of customers walked in, a family with two children.

"Yours," Nancy said to Molly.

"C'mon. You're training."

Nancy rolled her eyes and slid off the stool, motioning for Anne to follow. Chip wiped down the bar where they'd been sitting.

"Hey," Nancy said to the family. "Can I get you some drinks?" Anne thought that was rather abrupt. She would modify that, tell them her name perhaps.

"I'll have a Bud," said the father, looking down at his menu. The woman turned to her children. "Kids, what do you want to drink?"

"Coke," said one.

"No Coke today. Do you want water or milk?"

"Lemonade."

The woman turned to Nancy. "Two milks for them, please. And I'll have a Diet Coke. What's your soup today?"

"Beer cheese."

The woman looked displeased. "Hmm," she said, and turned back to her menu.

Nancy talked to Anne as she walked. "Milk sucks cuz you have to go to the basement to get it. Don't forget to grab plastic cups on the way down." She reached behind a stack of large light pink plastic cups at the waitress station and produced two small brown ones.

"Bud," she said to Chip, before walking downstairs to the large refrigerators. Anne followed, uncomfortable. She felt like a dog.

"Don't fill them too high or you'll jinx it and the kids'll spill." She screwed the cap back on the jug, and they headed back up the stairs.

"Trays are under here," she said, grabbing a brown saucer from the second shelf of the dish cart. She set the milks on the tray and added the beer Chip had waiting. Then she filled a pink plastic cup with ice—"Don't ever use a glass to do this," she said—and filled it with soda from the gun.

"Can we have straws?" asked the boy, when Anne and Nancy returned to the table.

"Sure, hon," said his mother, and she looked at Nancy.

Nancy walked back to the bar and grabbed two red drink straws. "Soda straws are too long for the kid cups," she told Anne, who was still following her like a backpack.

"I want a big one, with blue stripes," said the girl.

"Those are too big for your cup," Nancy explained.

"Mommy, can I have a big straw?"

"Sure. Say please."

The girl turned back to Nancy. "Can I have a big straw, *please*?"

Nancy pursed her lips and walked to the waitress station. She searched out two blue-striped straws and carried them balanced on a saucer back to the table.

"Are you ready to order?" she asked.

"You go first," the wife said to the husband.

"I'll have the cobb salad," he said. "No ham. Ranch on the side."

"Ohhh, you're being so good," said the wife. "I was going to get nachos. I guess I'll have the chicken sandwich, no mayo."

"Fries, chips, potato salad, or coleslaw?" said Nancy.

"Do you have anything else?" she asked.

"Side salad, for a dollar extra."

"I'll have that, ranch on the side."

"Okay. And you?" Nancy turned to the little boy.

"I want a grilled cheese."

"Fries, chips, potato salad, or coleslaw?"

"Fries."

"No fries," said the mother. She turned to Nancy. "He'll have potato salad."

Never mind, thought Anne, *that potato salad is loaded with the fattening mayonnaise you didn't want on your sandwich.*

Nancy turned to the little girl. "And you, honey?"

"A hamburger, please."

"Potato salad for her, too?" Nancy asked the mother.

"What are the choices again?"

"Fries, chips, potato salad, coleslaw."

"She'll try the coleslaw."

Nancy wrote on her pad. Several more people walked through the door. Nancy grabbed the menus from the family and brought them back to the cart by the waitress station where Molly was crouched over the bar, focused on a crossword.

"Table," said Nancy, and Molly straightened and reached inside her apron for pen and paper as she headed toward the customers.

Nancy tore the order from her pad and placed it on a clip in the kitchen window, then tapped the bell with her finger.

"They'll put the slip under a plate when the order is ready. Make sure to keep it because you have to turn in your orders at the end of the shift."

Anne had no idea how she would remember everything.

"Today'll be slow. Mondays always are," said Nancy, popping gum into her mouth and leaning back against the wall. Anne looked behind her through the open window into the small kitchen, where several men moved at a fast pace without bumping into each other or spilling anything. She thought of herself in her kitchen in Minnesota. She'd grown to enjoy cooking, especially baking, and felt much as these cooks looked—like she could make a lemon cake with her eyes closed, scraping a knife across the top of a measuring cup, tapping the metal sifter while the flour poured below, cracking an egg with one hand and releasing the yolk. Last Christmas, John bought her a set of Corelle mixing bowls in Spring Blossom Green, which she had admired in a catalog. She loved the feel of wiping batter away from the insides of the bowl with a rubber scraper, folding the batter over itself again and again. Early morning baking was her favorite, with John and Michael out performing chores and the light from the east pouring through the window above the sink. The smell of pines was strongest in the morning, as if the needles held on to their aroma during the cold of night and let it go as they warmed in the sun.

Nancy and Molly each had a few tables during the lunch hour, just enough to keep them busy but not enough to get what they called "the rush" of nonstop activity involved with taking care of up to ten tables at once.

"The Friday night rush is the best," said Molly, as she and Nancy took a cigarette break outside at two-thirty and Anne stood with them. "Before you know it, the night's over and you've made a hundred bucks."

"How much do you usually make during the day?" Anne asked.

"Depends. On a good day, you'll leave with fifty, maybe."

When John died, he and Anne still owed many thousands of dollars on the farm, including the house, equipment, and animals. She sold each piece for the highest price she could get and collected John's meager life insurance. After paying her debts and funeral expenses, she felt lucky to be left with a balance close to zero, and Michael's college fund untouched.

Anne figured if she worked Monday through Friday, she would have two hundred and fifty dollars a week in tips. That would be a thousand dollars a month, plus what she earned some Saturdays and her hourly wage of two dollars. But that was figuring on every day being a "good day." There was no way to know for sure, when she was dependent on tips, whether she would have enough every month. She would just have to wait and see.

Joe peeked around the corner of the fence blocking the outdoor waitress station from the patio where a few diners sat.

"Mind if I join you ladies?" he asked.

"Nope," said Nancy. She held out her pack of cigarettes, and Joe grabbed one. His hand looked rough, but newly so, Anne thought, as if it had just recently been put to work. His nails were white as clouds, though. He took great effort to look presentable; his face was scrubbed, hair combed, and clothes unstained, if slightly outdated. One had to look closely to see the frayed cuff on his left sleeve, the missing button on his pants, and the yellow ring on the inside of his collar. He had several nicks on his face from a razor he should have replaced several months ago. And his sandy hair was just a bit too long.

He extended a hand to Anne. "I'm Joe."

"Anne. Pleased to meet you."

The four of them stood together, quiet, for a few moments, and Anne's mind went to John, to his hands, one of the things she loved about him. The fingers were broad like him, strong. His hands were rough enough that when she ran her fingers along them, she felt protected. But they were soft enough that every callous did not scrape her skin. They were a farmer's hands and a husband's hands.

"Any luck?" Nancy was asking Joe.

"Naw. Not a bit." Joe shrugged his shoulders. "I'm too old."

"I'm sure something will come along," said Molly.

"No doubt," said Joe. "Say, did you know it's my birthday tomorrow? Seventy-five if I'm a day."

"Bullshit," said Nancy. "You don't look it."

"You're a liar, but thank you."

"I'll tell Debbie. We'll get a cake," said Molly.

"No, no. Debbie is no fan of mine."

"Well, I'll tell Kevin, then."

"No, just put a candle in my beer."

Nancy threw her cigarette in the bucket. "Speaking of, we've got to get back inside."

Kevin stood behind the bar with Chip, marking down inventory on the clipboard in his hand. He looked up as the women walked in and sat on the stools.

"I didn't know you smoked," he said to Anne.

"Oh, I don't. I was just along for the conversation."

"Now's the perfect time to give us the dish on Kevin," said Molly. She leaned her elbows on the bar and looked across Nancy to Anne. "I picture him a young kid walking around making money. Like Lucy in Charlie Brown." She giggled.

Anne shook her head. "I never would have thought he'd own restaurants."

"No?" asked Nancy.

"He was always so interested in science. He used to carry around tweezers and a baggie so he could take samples of things and look at them under his microscope."

"Oh, please tell us more," said Nancy. "What kinds of things?"

"Bits of dirt. Pennies. Hair. Anything, really. One time he had me stick out my tongue and put it under."

Chip turned to Kevin. "Do you still do stuff like that?"

Kevin looked at him sideways. "No."

"Where is the microscope?" asked Anne.

Kevin continued writing on his clipboard. "I have no idea."

"Remember when we were digging for samples and we found that skull?"

Nancy lit another cigarette. "No, shit?"

Anne nodded. "It was probably a raccoon or opossum. Remember, Kevin?"

He nodded as he continued counting bottles, and she turned back to Nancy.

"He hit himself in the face with the shovel, he was digging so furiously." She laughed. "See, there? That scar along his temple is from the shovel."

Kevin waved her away. "Alright, enough. I'll be in the office."

When he'd gone, Nancy leaned over and said, "Tell me this: Was he always so happy-go-lucky?"

"You don't know Kevin," Anne snapped.

Nancy held up her hands and turned to Molly and Chip. "Runs in the family, I guess."

At three fifteen, Michael walked in. Anne never saw a sweeter face. She walked to him and led him behind the wall to the waitress station. "What a nice surprise!"

"I came to walk you home," said Michael. And Anne had a flash, a memory drawn from so far back she could only assume she had saved it for this moment, a memory of John as a sixteen-year-old boy standing outside of the library where Anne worked every Saturday. She had to, according to her parents, for spending money. But Anne would have, anyway. The quiet suited her. And also the unassuming power of shelving and arranging the knowledge and wisdom, book by book, contained within.

John was a boy from class, and she sometimes sat with him in study hall, but they had never dated. "I'm here to walk you home," he said to her one summer afternoon as she left. He was unembarrassed, much unlike Anne imagined any of the other boys acting in such a circumstance. He said it simply, but with such seriousness and emotion that Anne felt she had been asked to marry him. And, looking back, she had.

Nancy and Molly appeared from their cigarette break. "Who is this little man?" asked Molly.

Anne put her arm around Michael's shoulders, partly out of pride but also to protect. She thought Michael might be shy and uncomfortable here, perhaps because she was.

"This is my son, Michael. He came to walk me home."

"Is it three-thirty already?" Nancy was quick to ask.

"Almost." Anne would be sure to stay until at least then.

At the end of her first day, Anne was happy to go home. She knew she would be able to do the job well, but she did not imagine she would find joy at work. Molly was sweet, but at such a different spot in life there was no hope of finding anything in common. Chip, she did not trust. And Nancy was like every waitress she'd ever come across—she swore, she smoked, she drank. Anne imagined that she spent many nights at bars or casinos, a schooled drinker, rarely sloppy. Never married. Children unwanted. She lived in an apartment or perhaps a trailer, maybe with a boyfriend. Anne could see it, clear as day.

Six

J ulia slipped her letter into a mailbox on her way to Ackerman Elementary School. Rose had not yet written or called. But then, Julia hadn't called either, and she did not plan to. She would wait for a letter, to see what Rose had to say. To know what she was thinking. The day she left, Julia had placed a note on the counter, a letter tightly sealed in an envelope. Julia remembered pushing down the seal with her fingers over and over, as if maybe Rose might never have to open it. In the letter, she'd tried to explain her belief that she was possibly doing something wrong by living with Rose. Being with Rose. That she believed she'd made a mistake, maybe. That she needed her own life for a while. To figure things out.

As Julia thought of the letter, walking to school, she knew she'd made the person she respected most in the world the object of her trite, meaningless words—words that totaled a mere three sentences. She didn't expect Rose would ever write to her.

She had been to the school twice before in the last week, once to drop off some of her things and once for orientation. She found the other teachers nice. Not overly-friendly. A bit wary, actually, especially the women, and it seemed to Julia that working at a school might be a bit like going to one. She knew she would have to earn their approval, if she cared to try. Which she did not. She was determined to keep her anonymity as best she could until she sorted herself out. She would throw herself into the one thing she knew she was meant to do: teach.

When she arrived, she stood in the doorway holding a final box of books and looked at her new classroom, letting it finally sink in that this was now hers. Rows of small desks faced the chalkboard, waiting for the little bodies that would sit and practice letters and multiplication, scratch names into the metal base with safety pins, and stick gum under the chairs. She smelled pencils and textbook pages and something like graham crackers. Julia smiled, feeling the warm embrace of an old friend.

The windows faced south. Julia had already placed a potted plant on the ledge there and filled the bookcase underneath with Beverly Cleary, C.S. Lewis, Judy Blume, and Mark Twain. She added a few Nancy Drew and Hardy Boys mysteries, as well as magazines and comic books. Julia had the controversial opinion that as long as a child was reading, it didn't much matter the content. She wanted to teach her students to love reading, and she'd do it by any means necessary.

Julia finished organizing her desk and looked at her watch. It was time to walk downstairs to the office of the principal, Don Ludlow.

"Just wanted to take a moment to see how you're settling in," he said, smiling.

"Fine, thank you."

"Where are you living?"

"In an apartment above Westway Drugs."

Ludlow raised his eyebrows. "We'll have to motion the board for a pay raise."

Julia laughed. "I like a bit of color in my life. It makes for conversation." She flinched to herself as she thought again of Rose, and it occurred to her that she liked color only in other people's lives.

"Well, we're glad you're here—glad, especially, to have filled the position so quickly. Should have known Rebecca wouldn't come back once her baby was born."

"I'm glad for it. " Julia smiled.

"I know it's your first year. If you have any questions, let me know. Or one of the other girls."

"I do have some ideas about group learning that I'd like to get your opinion on. And I noticed several books I would recommend are not on the reading list. How do I add them?"

"Easy there." He chuckled. "Rome wasn't built in a day." He stood, and he looked at Julia until she did the same.

"Well," he said, extending a hand, "I do hope you find yourself at home here."

The breeze was cool the first day of fourth grade, as if it too knew summer was over. Michael walked the block to his new school, stopping along the fences where impatiens grew to pop the buds. Except for those boys who had pushed him down that day he arrived, he would not know anyone. He'd always had friends. He didn't remember ever having to make any. But, still, he was looking forward to it. For Michael, school had always provided comfort. He loved the smell of pencils, the shiny smooth pages of books, and the lit classroom on dark, stormy mornings.

His mother had received a letter assigning Michael to Miss Julia Parnell's classroom. She was the new teacher, and Anne had said, "How fitting." The students filed into the classroom, buzzing like happy bees, all except Michael excitedly talking anew, though most of them had seen each other during the summer. Miss Parnell sat at her desk and smiled at each student. Michael was one of the few who held her eye contact and smiled back.

At his school in Minnesota, Michael's teacher was old. Her face was powdered with rouge that smelled sweet but was mixed with cigarette smoke, so it made Michael cough when she bent down over his desk. She had yellow teeth. When she was angry, she developed a brogue.

Miss Parnell was younger than his mom. She wore a striped pink dress that looked like a shirt on top. She had blonde hair that turned up slightly at the shoulders and blue eyes that sparkled out at him.

She held no book or tablet in her hand as she walked to the front of the classroom and sat on a stool and crossed her legs. She just clasped her hands in her lap and began talking to the children about what they were going to learn together this year. She even asked if anyone had anything to add to the list. None of the students were used to being asked what they wanted to learn, and so none of them raised their hands.

At recess, a circle formed around the tetherball. The children took turns slapping at the ball hanging from a rope. Michael had never played, but he stood in line anyway. And though no one talked to him, they smiled and offered the ball when it was his turn to face off against Jason Lutz, the reigning champion.

Jason stood on the other side of the pole and waited for Michael to hit the ball. His face showed no concern, for he'd been king of the tetherball since last year. He was confident he would continue to win until he lost interest in the game and deemed it boring. Most of the other children would lose interest then, too.

Michael steadied the ball in one hand and raised the other.

"Go on!" yelled Jason, startling Michael and causing the ball to roll from his hand and fall against the post.

"Ha! You lose!" yelled Jason.

"That's not fair," said Michael.

"Let him go again," said Ben.

Jason rolled his eyes, but his silence signaled acquiescence.

Michael slapped the ball hard. It swooped downward and then up, over Jason's head and back around to Michael, who hit it again. Jason slapped back, but Michael had the reflexes of a catcher-pitcher-shortstop all in one and had no problem preventing the tetherball from passing by him. It took only two more hits of the swinging ball before he had it wound all the way around the pole.

Jason looked angry for a moment, then swallowed.

"Good," he said. "I'm sick of this stupid game." He walked toward the monkey bars, and several boys followed.

The bell rang, making Michael the reining tetherball champion.

At the end of the day, Miss Parnell gave them an assignment. "Tell us something we don't know about you," she said. "Something you find interesting about yourself. Write a few lines, and bring it tomorrow."

Michael was excited. This was perfect; it was like they were all new students. And there was so much he could tell people. He could tell them about the wolves in Minnesota. He bet no one around here had ever seen a live wolf. He could tell them about searching for traps with his father, or about how in Minnesota, his father let him drive their truck. Or that last year he was elected president of his elementary student council, and he was only a third grader. He could tell them about how much he loved baseball. How every day during the summer in Minnesota, he and his friends went to a field and played; how once he hit a home run batting right and the next inning he hit a home run batting left. How he knew the names and stats of every Chicago Cub going back five years, because their radio in Minnesota carried WGN—maybe that would win them over, that he knew about their home team.

But he decided to tell them he was adopted. This was, he thought, the most interesting thing about him. He had grown up reading a book called *Why Was I Adopted?* and learned that adoption made him different in a good way. That another person happened to deliver him at the hospital, but the Nygaards were his parents. Being adopted made him special, exotic even. It wasn't often that Michael thought about being adopted, but when he did, he was proud in the same way he was proud of the scar on his forehead he got from falling off the top branch of the crabapple tree in Pike's yard, when he landed on a stick on the ground.

That night, Michael lay on his stomach on the floor, writing in his school notebook while his mother read on the couch. They had spent many evenings like this in Minnesota, with his father reading the *Farmer's Almanac* in a chair. When Michael finished his homework, they'd switch on the television. Most times they agreed on a program, but every Wednesday night, without fail, his mother argued for *Alice* and his father for *The Fall Guy*. They went back and forth in their quiet but stubborn way before settling. Michael was always impatient with these arguments. Now he wished to hear them again.

The olive carpet scratched his elbows as he wrote. It occurred to Michael that had another family adopted him, he might still have a father. But the thought slipped back out of his mind. He didn't want another father alive. He wanted his father.

After several minutes in the clearing, as they waited for the wolves to appear, Michael's father began to talk. "The hillside faces south. That way, the wolves get some warmth from the sun even in winter." John's breath misted around his face and trailed upward. "There won't be any pups right now, it's too early. It's still mating season, though, so they're active." As he spoke, his eyes remained on the hillside. "Wolves mate for life. They stay together until one of them dies."

He took two cheese sandwiches wrapped in wax paper out of his pocket and handed one to Michael, who held it in his lap with both hands.

"Did I ever tell you your grandmother hunted wolves?" John asked.

Michael's eyes widened. "No."

John shook his head. "That woman. She was a pilot, which was rare in those days. A big to-do was made, and she was in the paper. Anyway, the Depression came and she got the notion she'd hunt wolves for money. Government paid $15 for females, less for males and pups. You could make four hundred dollars a winter, and she often did. Hunting wolves from the air wasn't easy, but it was easier than tracking them on the ground. You could come across a dozen or more wolves in the wide-open space of a frozen lake, and two shooters could down four or five of them within seconds. After a week, they'd have enough wolves to drape over the entire plane, wings and all. I've seen photos in your grandma's old albums."

"She shot enough wolves to cover a whole plane?"

"Sure did."

Michael thought he saw something like pride in his father's eyes. "But you hate hunting wolves."

"Your grandmother was a young woman, not even twenty. And I guess I can't speak to it. I've never been dirt poor. She helped feed her family. But what they're doing here," he waved his arm to cover the forests, "that's not for survival. And we've learned some since the '20s. We've learned that bounties get things out of balance in ways we didn't understand. We've learned there are other options to keep wolves from eating livestock."

"Like not leaving the dead ones out in the woods."

"Right. And bringing them in at night. Training dogs. Using electronics to scare the wolves. All kinds of things."

"Why don't they do that?"

"Money is part of it," said John. "And those methods don't always work." He took a bite of his sandwich. "But mostly I think it's change. People don't like it. You're raised hating wolves, you'll die hating wolves."

"But why?"

"It's never made much sense to me, either. They're wild animals, we're smarter than they are. Seems it's up to us to figure out how to live with them."

Michael thought about this. He looked down at the uneaten sandwich in his lap. "But we hunt," he said.

His father nodded, understanding. "It's how humans have survived. It isn't needless."

"But we can go to the store."

"Not for deer or pheasant, we can't. And I'd rather take my own animal and use as much of it as I can than buy from some of these factory farms popping up all over the place." Michael knew many other farmers thought his father had unusual ideas, talking about organic and natural and humane treatment of animals. These farmers were not necessarily inhumane, but they were practical, hardened. They saw a very clear and very thick line between human and animal. Michael remembered once his father coming home with tears in his eyes as he told his wife and son that he and a neighbor had found a young pig that had been partially skinned alive. The neighbor, just as concerned as John, took the pig to his farm and began the necessary procedures to try to salvage some of the skin, snip off other bits, and wrap the wounds. The pig was in obvious distress.

"Shouldn't we call the vet for anesthesia?" asked John, to which the neighbor responded, "It's a pig, John."

But John had never believed animals felt less. In fact, being raised on a fox farm had made him more sensitive. His great-grandfather, arriving from Norway with the tradition in his pocket, bought his first four foxes within days of landing, and John's grandfather and father had continued raising, breeding, and harvesting the descendants of those four. When demand for fox fur declined as it went out of fashion, John's father bought minks. Women's fashion kept the farm in business—if not thriving, certainly stable. But when John inherited the farm, he'd had enough of raising, killing, and skinning animals. He took the minks to a refuge, tore down the pens, and planted soybeans.

Michael bit into his sandwich as his father continued watching the hillside.

"You know," said John, "wolves' instincts are so keen, they often know which in a herd of animals is sick. They know, even before they start running, which animal they're going after."

Michael nodded, thought about this as he chewed. "Maybe they take the sick cattle from Mr. Ebersold's herd. Maybe they're doing him a favor."

His father chuckled. "I wouldn't be surprised." He picked at his eyebrow and nodded toward the hill. "There's six of them, now that the grandmother is gone. The alpha male is a funny old guy. I once saw him pick up a mound of snow with his snout and toss it in his companion's face. He was playing! The alpha female is all business, keeping an eye out while the others play. She's darker than the alpha male, almost black. There are two younger females, born last year. The grandmother raised them, stuck by the den and never left with the others. They're already skilled hunters. I almost saw those two take down a coyote late last fall, but they ran into the trees over there."

"Wolves eat coyotes?" asked Michael.

"No, not usually. But they'll chase one out of their territory. I think those juveniles were just testing their skills. And then there are what I think of as the alpha's brothers, two males. One of them is the omega."

"How do you know?"

"He's submissive. The others nip and bare their teeth at him. He's fairly big, but you don't have to be the smallest to be the omega."

"Why doesn't he leave?" asked Michael. He threw a bit of crust off into the forest for the squirrels.

"Sometimes an omega will do that. But it's safer to be with a pack. Another pack might kill a lone wolf that comes into their territory."

"Gosh," said Michael. "Kill it?"

"They have to," said his father. "It's not just a matter of space and land and this is mine and this is yours. It's a matter of survival, of family. If other wolves hunt on their territory, they have less to eat. Less to feed their mates, less to feed their pups. The pack could perish."

But Michael was saddened. His teacher at school had once said that an animal's only aim was to survive. Every decision was based on it. It wasn't even a decision, really. Just instinct, pure and unhindered. Michael knew this was right, the way things should be. And yet the cruelty of the animal world he so loved often startled him.

Seven

M iss Parnell's students came to class with their finished papers and were relieved when Michael raised his hand to go first.

"Yes, Michael," said Miss Parnell. "Please go ahead."

Michael tried to contain his smile as he walked to the front of the classroom. He faced everyone and held his notebook paper with both hands. "Something you don't know about me is that I was adopted. When I was born, my mother was only sixteen. She and her parents decided that she was too young to take care of me. She needed to go to high school. So my parents, Anne and John Nygaard, decided to adopt me."

Most of the children stared at Michael from their desks. They stopped swinging their feet and shuffling their own papers. Michael glanced briefly at his classmates before continuing with the final lines.

"*Adopt* means that my parents took care of me and made me their own son. It makes me different in a good way." He was unsure whether he should have included that last line because it seemed like bragging. He wished he wouldn't have let his mother put it in there.

"Thank you, Michael," said Miss Parnell, with a smile. "That was very good. Please have a seat."

Michael walked back to his desk and sat down. The girl in front of him turned and whispered, "My cousin is adopted. My dad says that her real mom was a druggie. Was your mom a druggie?"

"No," said Michael.

"My dad says that my cousin never really belonged in our family. You can tell by her freckles and the way she laughs like a pig."

"I don't have freckles," said Michael, but he was already feeling less proud.

The girl turned back around as another student began her report. Student after student rose and walked to the front of the room, but Michael only heard bits and pieces about favorite colors, swimming, and doing wheelies.

At recess, Michael again joined the crowd at the tetherball. He was a few seconds late, however, and two children were already playing. No one moved to allow Michael to regain his place at the top of the tetherball hierarchy. A few girls whispered among a large group of children from Michael's class. They laughed together and kept their backs to Michael, who stood on the outside of the circle, waiting for a turn to play.

Suddenly, a soccer ball hit Michael in the temple, and he stumbled backward onto his bottom. Someone laughed and soon none of the other children could help it, either. But they overdid it, buckling and holding their stomachs. Look at him, fallen backward on the pavement. What a stupid, silly fool.

The soccer ball rolled to Jason's feet, and he kicked it back at Michael. It hit his nose, and blood flowed onto his upper lip.

"Stay back!" yelled Jason. "He's a bastard! He could have AIDS!" All the children flew away, squealing and laughing, though most of them did not know what a bastard was.

Michael knew. He ran toward the school doors, away from the children and the circle of teachers chatting near the monkey bars at the far end of the playground. He could not understand why his parents had lied to him, why his mother didn't warn him that people would make fun of him. He found refuge in the last stall in the boys' bathroom and cried. Maybe he hadn't realized that being adopted was shameful, but now he understood.

As Michael walked home from school that day, he thought about how to tell his mother what had happened. He was embarrassed and ashamed, but still he had the urge to tell, to let her make it better.

But when he walked in the door, his mother sat on the couch, crying into her hands. She looked up with soaked eyes.

"Oh, my goodness," she said, rising as she wiped her cheeks and smoothed her slacks. "Is it three thirty?"

Michael stood silent at the front door. He wanted to ask her what was wrong but, without knowing it, took his mother's cue and said nothing.

"Let me get you some apples and milk," she said.

Michael made his way to the kitchen as Anne began slicing an apple on their old wooden cutting board. Michael stopped and looked at it, remembered his father had made it. On the underside, he'd carved, "J + A." His mother had giggled when he gave it to her.

Michael went to the refrigerator, wanting to help her.

"No, no. Sit down. I'll get it," she said. "How was your report? Tell me."

"It was fine. Really good. The teacher loved it."

"That's wonderful, Michael."

She kissed his temple as she placed down the plate of apple slices. "We are going to be fine here, you and I."

It was the first time Michael did not believe something his mother said.

The next day, Michael was scared to go to school. This was a new feeling. But when he arrived, no one much looked at him. Maybe, Michael hoped, they'd forgotten what Jason said.

All morning, the children worked. They spoke to Michael while solving math problems or discussing reading questions in small groups as Miss Parnell glided around the classroom, listening. Jason ignored him. Michael felt more and more at ease, relaxed into the hard plastic of his chair.

At recess, he sat against the brick wall and watched a four-square game. This game, too, was new to Michael, and he thought it looked very fun. He tried to figure out all the rules as he watched from the side. Four children, each in a quarter of a large square, bounced a ball back and forth until someone made a mistake, and then they were out. One of the several children waiting in line would then get a turn and fill the square. You couldn't catch or hold the ball too long, and the bounce had to be within the lines. This much Michael knew.

The children paid him no attention, and their indifference was a relief for now. Michael smiled to himself whenever a particularly tough pass was achieved, and at one point, when Jason missed the ball, Michael let out an involuntary groan.

Jason glared at Michael from where he stood, having paused the game. "Go away!" he yelled, but Michael did not move.

Jason charged over.

"I said, go away! What are you, retarded?"

Michael said nothing, so Jason kicked his shoe.

"Are you retarded?"

"No," said Michael.

A wall of boys and girls watched.

"He says he's not retarded," Jason said to them. "He must be retarded, to hang out by himself at recess." He turned back to Michael and mocked him in the thick, deep voice he had heard from his neighbor with Down's syndrome. "Are. You. A. Retard?" He twisted his hands and fingers in his own grotesque version of sign language and let his tongue hang from his mouth. Some of the other children laughed. The rest just looked. Here was an unfamiliar boy sitting in front of them—not only new, but also adopted. They didn't know what to do.

"Stop it," said Michael.

"I'm Michael," continued Jason. "I'm a retard."

The bell rang. The children, including Jason, turned and ran from Michael, discarding him as quickly as they would a used napkin.

Eight

Dear Rose,

I may have overreached with my assignment to the children. A boy named Michael used the assignment to tell the class—proudly, mind you—that he is adopted. The children—the wonderful, horrible, sweet, brutal children—have been just cruel to him. And he is such an endearing boy, always polite. Quick to offer a pencil or paper if someone doesn't have it.

I thought maybe I should have a lesson on acceptance, but then would that be targeting him yet again? None of the other children have been made fun of for their speeches—no one actually had anything interesting to say, except Michael.

It's comforting, in a way. We all come from the same beginning. We have the same needs. What's discomforting is the thousands of directions we can go. The thousands of ways we can be ruined by other people and other things. I hope to encourage the good I see and reverse the bad. But, oh, children can be cruel. Adults, too, but we have manners, and so we mask our cruelty in other things. Children have not yet learned that art, and so their cruelty can be startling.

Please write.

Julia

Julia had begun filling her letters with all the details of her life without Rose. She shared and shared these details, describing her students, especially Michael, their habits and mannerisms, their favorite subjects, the other teachers, the playground dramas, her apartment, town, and neighbors. Each detail an effort to feel close with Rose without having to be. Her sadness spread to include Michael, and she wanted Rose to know.

Michael was unaware that Miss Parnell's eyes followed him, that she saw his ostracism, no matter how quiet it was in the classroom. Children have such a narrow view of things, without any idea how much the adults around them see of their little worlds. He was unaware that she saw him sit at the fence during recess, far across the playground, knew he was reading books about wolves. She watched him day after day, a book resting on his knees, head down. He didn't know she asked the librarian to stock more books about the animals. He didn't know Miss Parnell saved magazines with wolf articles, searched them out, even stole one from the dentist's office.

And when Miss Parnell's science unit on birds was cut short and she introduced a unit on *Canis lupus*, Michael was pleased that the stars had aligned, unaware that his teacher had stayed up past midnight four nights in a row to learn enough about the animal to teach the class.

She ached to comfort Michael, to let him shine in front of the other students. She asked him to read a paragraph, then called on him to answer three of the first six questions, even when he didn't raise his hand. Quiet at first, Michael became animated. He answered the questions and then extrapolated on memories of Minnesota, the woods, his father. He raised his hand as another student stumbled through an answer, the wrong answer, and soon the other students were not so much impressed as annoyed.

Julia sensed this, but too late. She tried to regain control.

"You've *seen* a wild wolf, Michael? How cool!" she said, too excited. This did not help.

One day, two weeks into the year, as the class dissected the owl pellets they were supposed to before the wolf unit, Julia listened to three of her female students giggle about a new boy in fourth grade. Michael, sitting at the next table over, looked giddy.

"What's his name?" he asked, and the three girls looked at him, unaware he'd been listening.

"Peter," said Jenny, and she turned back to her friends.

Something flicked at Julia's heart.

She followed the children outside at recess and wandered behind Michael. First he asked Jenny to point out the new boy, then he walked over to where Peter sat alone on the blacktop. As Julia strolled, she watched Michael extend his hand. The boy took it, squinting upward.

"I'm Michael," Julia heard.

"I know," said Peter.

Michael looked pleased. "And your name's Peter."

Peter nodded.

Michael pointed to the too-big Spider Man watch circling Peter's wrist. "Like Spider Man."

Peter shrugged.

Julia moved away toward the monkey bars, too nervous for Michael to listen any longer. When she looked back, she saw Jason Lutz grab Peter's hand and pull him away to a kickball game. And the thing that had been flicking at Julia's heart grabbed hold and squeezed.

Michael sat alone for a moment, then walked to Julia. They stood together awhile, watching the girls and boys run zigzag around them.

"Miss Parnell, what is AIDS?"

She looked down at the top of Michael's head. "It's a sickness."

"Like a cold?"

"Well, sort of, but a lot worse. You can die from it."

"How do you get it?"

"No one is exactly sure all the ways you can get it, but you have to be in close contact with someone who has it."

"Like playing at recess together?"

"No, you can't get it from playing together."

"Like sneezing on them?"

"They don't think so, no."

"Can you get it from being adopted?"

She knelt down. "Oh, honey, no," she said. "You can't get it from being adopted."

"Everyone says so."

"They don't understand what they're saying."

"But what if I got it from my birth mom? I don't even know her."

"You would know by now. You don't have AIDS, and you especially don't have AIDS just because you are adopted."

The bell rang. They waited for the mobs of children to leave the playground and then walked into the building together.

"Class, settle down," said Julia. "Please take out your social studies books and turn to page sixteen. Andrew, please stay in your seat. Thank you. Jenny, no markers. Michael, I'd like you to read, please. Start at the top."

"Can retards even read?" snickered Jason to the boy in front of him.

Julia slammed her book shut, and the class froze. They watched as she continued in a steady voice.

"Jason, if you are unwilling to act with decency like a proper human being, I will send you to the principal's office and continue to send you there every day until the end of the year. You will have no recess, you will eat lunch by yourself, and you will do your work alone. Do you understand?"

Jason's eyes welled with tears. "Yes, Miss Parnell."

Julia tried to speak with the principal, tried to get someone to do something about the way Michael was being treated. She appealed to Claudia O'Neil, the fifth grade teacher who often supervised recess with her. But no one listened, and behind her back, they called her a softy.

"It's just kid stuff," said Claudia.

Instead, toward the end of the first month of school, it was Julia who was called into the principal's office. Bob Ludlow felt he had to respond to a complaint from Jason Lutz's parents.

"Did you say he wasn't human?"

"No," said Julia. "Not exactly. I said he was not acting like a proper human being. He was mocking a boy in class."

Ludlow sighed. "Michael Nygaard?"

"Yes."

"I'm confident he and the other boys just need time to adjust." He smiled.

"I think we need a policy on bullying."

"A policy on bullying?" Ludlow laughed. "What would that be, exactly? That kids shouldn't be kids? No jokes? No teasing?"

Julia started to answer, but he picked up his blinking telephone to signal the meeting was over.

Nine

After Miss Parnell yelled at Jason, instead of reading, Michael asked to go to the bathroom, where he sat in the last stall. He felt very alone, as if the rest of the world danced in happiness around him, oblivious to the child curled up in a ball in the center. His mother had her own sadness, but even if she did not, he decided he wouldn't tell her. He didn't want her to find out that her only child, the one someone else picked for her, was an embarrassment.

Michael had found a spot under a large, spreading maple in the back corner of the schoolyard and sat with his back against the chain-link fence each day during recess. No one talked to him. No one bothered him. He became okay with this, for then he could read or think about his father. Besides Miss Parnell, there wasn't anyone he wanted to talk to, anyway.

Miss Parnell was turning out to be a teacher unlike any other he'd had. The other day, she even had them stand at their desks and stretch, then jump up and down and yell. Principal Ludlow stuck his head in the door, but Miss Parnell assured him everything was okay.

"That might be so in here, Miss Parnell," he said. "But the other teachers are distracted."

Michael had never heard a teacher get in trouble before, and he looked at Miss Parnell. But she just smiled and put her hair behind her ear and said, of course, they would quiet down.

Under his tree one day, Michael poked the shell of a cicada with a stick, and it crunched in a satisfying way. The crumbs sprinkled down to the soil where the maple's roots pushed up and then went down deep again. He'd heard a tree's roots went down as far as the branches went up and thought of the storm last summer that pushed over one of the Mulvey oaks. That wind could be stronger than a tree was something Michael could not grasp.

He looked up and watched the leaves like hands shading him from the sun and was reminded suddenly of a moment when he was small, very small, holding his mother's hand and looking up at her, seeing only her dark silhouette and the sun's bright rays shooting out around her. He wanted to be that small again. Soon, the leaves would fall and someone would rake them away and haul them off in black plastic bags. Michael imagined them sitting atop a garbage heap rotting in the sun, so far from home. He decided to stay all winter and sit under his tree, waiting for new leaves to grow.

"Hey."

Michael turned to see a girl crouching on the other side of the fence. She wore turquoise stretch pants and a long, pink shirt all knotted down the sides. Black jelly bracelets laced her skinny wrists, and her dark hair was feathered at the ears.

"I can't stand recess, either," she said. "Bunch of babies running around like monkeys. It's so gay. I'm kind of new, too, so I don't really know anyone, either. At least, that's what I figure—that you sit here under this tree because you don't know anyone. I go to the junior high," she said, thumbing behind her. "Sixth grade. You must be younger. What's the matter? Don't you talk?"

Michael had been watching the words pour out of her mouth. He looked up to her eyes and noticed they were green. "Fourth grade," he said. "I'm in fourth grade."

"Where'd you come from?"

"Minnesota."

"Cool beans. I'm from Wisconsin." She extended an index finger through the fence. "Tina."

He took it. "Michael."

"I don't like it at all so far. Do you?" she asked.

"No. I want to go back."

"How come? I don't like it, either, but Milwaukee wasn't any better. No place is."

"Minnesota is."

"Why?"

"We had animals and a farm."

"Well," she said. "There's a petting zoo coming next week." She glanced at her hands and bit at a hangnail. "I do miss my boyfriend," she said, her teeth clenched around some skin.

"You had a boyfriend?"

"His name was Scott. He was fourteen." She spat skin onto the grass. "Have you kissed anyone?"

Michael blushed. "No."

"You should," Tina said. "It's fun. I've seen my parents kiss. With tongue. I've even seen them in their bed together. They don't always close the door all the way."

Michael chuckled.

"Do you know what the swearword for sex is?" Tina asked.

"Yes."

"Say it."

"You say it."

"Fuck. Say it."

Michael hesitated. "Fuck."

Tina smiled. Michael realized suddenly she was the girl who stared out her window that first day he pulled up with his mother.

"I think you live across the street from me," he said.

"Yeah."

"You knew that? Why didn't . . ."

But Tina just stood and smiled and then ran off back to her school, joining the other children streaming into its doors as the bell rang.

Michael was happy as he walked toward his own school. He might have made a friend.

That afternoon, Tina waited outside for him after school.

"I know a way we can make some money for candy," she said without preface, as though he'd been expecting her.

They picked up the whirly-birds fallen from the maple trees in front of the school and stopped at each house on the way home, selling the seeds to their neighbors for ten cents. "Plant them in wet dirt, and soon you'll have a tree," Tina said, as Michael stood smiling by her side. The neighbors grinned and offered money.

After ten minutes, Tina split the dimes evenly, and they walked to the newsstand in town. When they pushed open the large glass door, the old lady behind the counter smiled at them with a cigarette between her lips.

"Hi, kiddos," she said, throaty and full of phlegm, the kind of voice one could swim through.

The small store stretched back from the entrance. The two long walls on either side were lined with magazines and romance novels. The front wall to the right of the door held stacks of newspapers and to the left, candy—racks of Mars, Snickers, M&Ms, Necco wafers; bins of Swedish fish, Tootsie Rolls, Bull's Eyes. The floor tiles were an indistinguishable color, possibly beige. Many were chipped at the corners to reveal the hardened glue underneath. The one at the door was worn to a slate-colored sheen from the thousands of first steps inside the store, mostly by men in dress shoes seeking the morning paper before they rode the train.

Tina wanted a pack of candy cigarettes, but they were fifty cents and she had only forty. Michael put back two of his Bull's Eyes and gave her a dime. He was walking toward the counter, candy in hand, when he saw it—a wolf staring out at him from a new *National Geographic*. Michael stood in front of it and looked at the black eyes and gray fur, so much like the wolves from home. The librarian never let him take the magazines out of the library. Now he could have his own, and it could always be with him.

"I don't have three dollars," he said over his shoulder to the cashier.

"Put back your candy," she said.

"But that'll only give me forty cents."

The woman looked at Tina.

"He'll still only have eighty," said Tina.

"Consider it a down payment," said the lady. "Come back with the money tomorrow."

Michael ran home hugging the magazine to his chest.

"Chill out," said Tina, trying to keep up. "I wanted candy. You owe me."

Michael didn't respond, just kept running, anxious to be reading the magazine.

"Let's do something," said Tina, when they arrived on their block.

"I think I'm just gonna go home," said Michael.

Tina rolled her eyes and headed to her house.

The message machine blinked—Michael's mother would be home at five o'clock, she said. She'd been staying the full shift more frequently because she said they needed the extra few dollars the time gave her. Michael took the magazine to the small room where they watched television and lay on the olive green carpet, flipping through the pages of wolf photographs. He wanted desperately to be able to show his father. He found and dog-eared several pages anyway.

"These are just like the wolves in Minnesota," he said aloud, and his father replied, "I miss you." Michael smiled and heard it again. "I miss you."

He looked up and could see his father sitting on the couch, an ankle resting on his knee. His elbow would be on the arm of the couch, his index and middle fingers holding up his head at the temple. This was how he sat watching television or, more often, reading.

When he heard the front door open, Michael jumped up and ran to the front room, almost expecting to see his father.

"Hi, Mom." Michael followed his mother to the kitchen and sat at the table watching her prepare dinner. His father stayed with him, and Michael imagined she was speaking to both of them when she talked.

"I feel like I'm in a different world at work," she said. "It's nice to be home."

"Do you like it?" asked Michael, or maybe his father.

"I'm catching on. Everyone is nice . . ." Her hand paused on the gas knob before continuing to move deftly about the stove. She shrugged. "These things just take time. I'm sure you feel the same at school."

She placed a loaf of French bread into the oven and turned to him. "What did you do after school?"

"Went to the candy store with Tina."

"Who's Tina?"

"She lives across the street."

Anne raised her eyebrows. She didn't even know a girl lived across the street. She hadn't talked to any neighbors since Mrs. Wilderhausen came with her muffins.

"Well, I'm glad," she said. "I'll try to get a firmer schedule so you'll know ahead of time which days I won't be here for you."

Michael opened the magazine at the table and looked at the wolves, calming instantly.

Tina sat with Michael at recess most days, though once in a while, she ignored Michael altogether and played in her own schoolyard with the "babies." Michael sat under his tree every day.

She did wait for him after school each afternoon, and they walked the block home together, or took their time the long way, making a large rectangle from school, through town, and back home. Tina was not much like Michael, and he was not sure he liked her. In Minnesota, Michael had played with boys who also worked on farms and loved baseball. They'd known him since he was a baby. They never rolled their eyes or raised their eyebrows at him, not seriously anyway. But, he recognized that this was a new life, with new people. Michael was walking through each day moment by moment. He felt a weight that made it hard, but he was walking, heading straight through, as his mother said they must. Tina always smiled when she saw him. Some of it was good.

"Spit out the seeds," Michael said to her one day as they walked home, eating slices of watermelon he had left over from lunch.

"Obviously."

"Has it ever happened to you?"

"What?"

"Did a watermelon ever grow in your stomach?"

"What are you talking about?"

"If you swallow a seed."

"Dummy. That can't happen."

Michael thought. He'd heard it could happen, but he supposed he'd never thought more about it, just took it as fact.

Tina threw her rind into someone's bushes.

"I'm an only child, too," she said, out of the blue. "But I guess I have a dad."

"Yeah." Michael was unsure how to respond, as he often was when Tina talked.

"I know!" Tina stopped walking and turned toward Michael. "Let's be blood brother and sister." She grabbed his hand and pulled him down the street to her house. In the kitchen, she grabbed a needle from the junk drawer.

Holding his hand, she pricked his finger and then hers. They mashed the blood together and she said, "There. It's forever." She took two bottles of Coke from the refrigerator. "Now let's go out-side. I have a secret to show you."

Michael let Tina pull him to the corner of the backyard, her arm lined with the black jelly bracelets she never took off. Tina lifted her T-shirt, with a picture of The Police on the front, to reveal a blue butterfly on her stomach.

"It's a tattoo," she said.

"It's not real." Michael took a sip of his Coke.

"Yes, it is. I took the train to the city yesterday."

"They wouldn't do it without your mom."

"How do you know? You just have to ask right."

"Did it hurt?"

"Nope, not at all. I might get another one. No, don't touch it," she said, as Michael reached with his fingers. "It's still sore."

"I thought you said it didn't hurt."

"It hurts after, dummy. It takes a few days to heal."

Michael turned to go. "Let's catch bees."

"Wait," said Tina. "Do you want one?"

"What?"

"A tattoo. For being blood brother and sister. We could each have one."

"No."

"We could take the train to the city together."

"No. I don't want one."

"You're such a baby."

Michael poured his remaining pop in the grass and went to the side garden full of blue cornflowers and catmint. Fat bumblebees floated lazily from flower to flower. Michael stuck his bottle next to a cornflower and waited.

"C'mon," said Tina. "Let's do something else."

"Shhh." A bee landed on the rim of Michael's bottle and seemed to consider whether to enter. Michael waited. Finally, the bee moved up inside the bottle, and Michael capped off the opening with his hand. He held the bottle in front of his face and looked, his large brown eyes peering in at the bee.

"They're pretty, aren't they?" said Michael. But Tina was concentrating on her own bottle. A bumblebee floated around the opening and landed but wouldn't go inside. It circled the rim, stopping for sips of leftover sugar. Tina couldn't wait, so she pushed the bee in with her palm and closed the opening.

"Ha!" she said. Her bottle still had too much Coke at the bottom, and the bee was having trouble getting out of it. Tina watched as the bee rose a bit, then fell back down into the sugary soda, rose, and fell again. It eventually found its footing on the sticky side of the bottle, but Tina shook the bottle, and the bee was back at the bottom, swimming. When Tina became bored, she tipped the bottle over, and the bee slid out onto the ground. It was soaking wet and stumbling among the blades of grass. Tina flicked the bee with her fingers until it landed on the cement patio. She crouched and watched as the bee tried to lift up and fly away, but its wings were weighed down. Finally, Tina stood and stepped on the bee, feeling the pop of the fat body under her gym shoe.

"Look," she called to Michael, and she pointed to the bee carcass.

"Why did you do that!"

"I had to, it was dying."

Michael released his bumblebee and dropped the bottle. "I have to go."

Michel swept the cement floor under the carport after dinner, a chore he completed with enjoyment, for it reminded him of sweeping out the barn at home. There were so few chores to do now it was hard to fill time. He had seen some neighbors with blowers removing leaves from their driveways and sidewalks and pushing them onto the street. He did not see the point in that, the leaves resting on the curb waiting for the next breeze. How did one sweep the earth?

"Hi, Michael." Tina stood before him on the driveway. "Can I help?" She picked up the dustpan and walked toward him. "I'm sorry I killed the bumblebee. I thought I was helping it." Tina looked at Michael, but he just pushed the broom back and forth across the concrete floor.

"My mom said you could come over for dinner tomorrow. We're

having hamburgers." She placed the dustpan on the floor, and Michael swept in the dirt and debris.

"Do you want to come?" asked Tina.

"Okay."

Tina smiled, relieved. "I was thinking. I know a way to get back at the kids at school."

"What?"

"We get them all on the playground—we'll tell them there's free ice cream or something—then we turn a pack of wolves on them. Or Jason from *Friday the 13th*."

Michael laughed. "*All* the kids aren't bad."

"We'll do the teachers, too."

"Except for Miss Parnell."

Tina rolled her eyes and threw her hand to her forehead. "Oh! Miss Parnell, you are so beautiful. My eyes cannot stand it. They are on fire! On fire!"

Michael blushed and shoved her. "Shut up. That not why I like her."

"But you do think she's beautiful."

He shrugged. "She's not ugly."

Tina smiled and shoved him back. "Don't you like any girls your own age?"

"Who is there to like? I don't know anyone."

"You know me, silly," she said, which was followed by silence. "I'm too old for you, anyway. You're practically my little brother." She put down the dustpan and skipped off. "See you tomorrow."

Ten

Tina's parents, Jim and Cassie Clark, met at eighteen and married three months later at a chapel in Las Vegas. Cassie gave up her immediate plans of going to college and supported Jim by cutting hair while he got his associate's degree and then entered the police academy in Milwaukee, their hometown. They loved each other for the first couple of years—madly, even. She was achingly attracted to Jim—his hair and eyes so black she almost felt naughty. And often, he could be sweet. Jim would buy shiny colored rocks from the hippie down the street while she was at work and leave one under her pillow before his night shift so she found it when she went to sleep. No one had ever done anything like that for her before, and she imagined the time and thought that it took. She had a collection of four tall, round glass vases, and she planned to fill them with the rocks and place the rainbow-ed vases in a row on the dresser along with her other rainbow things—a glass unicorn jumping over a rainbow, a small rainbow needlepoint she made for herself, a small bowl of rainbow paper roses.

She found she was good at cutting hair. Her client list grew so long that one day, as she sat on her chair at the salon, pushing herself in circles, the idea struck her that she was happy. It wasn't something she was moving toward anymore—away from the near-north side toward Whitefish Bay, away from rusted chain-link fences and tall dandelions toward square hedgerows and little signs speared into lawns warning of recent herbicide applications.

She had a cozy apartment, a husband, a little daughter in elementary school, and a job she was good at. And though she'd never imagined herself the type of person who could own a business, she decided right then on her chair that she would open her own salon. She had enough clients; all she needed to do was save money to rent a little space and buy some equipment. All of a sudden, it seemed easy.

In her memory, she decided to become an entrepreneur, Jim decided they would move, and the rocks stopped coming all at the same time. She wasn't sure these things happened together, but she felt it. Cassie called him with the news of her dream—or maybe he called her with the news of the move—and he said, "Well, just find some more clients in Illinois."

But the rocks stopped coming, too, at only two and a half vases full, and without that man beside her, the rock man, she had no desire to own a salon. She didn't want to be some single mother paying bills on the kitchen table at midnight, seeing her daughter only in the late, exhausted hours when all she wanted to do was watch television. No, Cassie wanted a husband, a family, and then a cute little salon. She wanted back that feeling she'd had on the chair. And so their marriage became a project for Cassie, because she did not have the courage to let it fail.

She could always remember that moment spinning in her chair when all the pieces seemed to fall together, but sometimes she could even feel it. And when she felt it, it was almost unbearable. Those were the days she took Tina into her room and cried to her. Because it reminded her that she was losing, that her life was still different from her dream, a dream she hadn't known was there until she felt it once, briefly, before it fluttered away.

Their only child, Christina May, was a brighter spot in her life, not as dull as the surrounding space. When she had a hard day at work dealing with bratty kids who wouldn't sit still and old men with dandruff, it was Tina who wrapped her arms around her mother. When Cassie fought with Jim, Tina brought her tissue from the bathroom.

"Divorce is not an option," Cassie would say often. "Plus, you'd resent us." She'd blow her nose into a tissue, loud like a horn. She seemed to know how to play this part, to skim the layers of emotion and understanding she'd seen on television, unaware that there was more—that when it was real, it was different.

"I don't know," Tina would say. She knew only that she wanted her parents to quit using her to say things to each other like, "Go ask your father why he hasn't mowed the lawn yet." And she wanted the three of them to do all the errands together on Saturdays, instead of going separately.

"If Jim could just remember what it used to be like."

"Used to be like when?"

"When we first met."

"Before me?"

"Partly. But you're not why we fight. We fight because, well, it's complicated. Maybe he's not in love with me anymore." She'd blow her nose again and sigh. "There's a reason he fell in love. I just need to remind him." She'd stroke Tina's hair with the long red nails of her thumb, ring, and pinky fingers, careful to keep her cigarette up and away, and say, "Oh, pumpkin, thanks for listening."

Jim Clark was a man's man. It was a choice, an angry choice. He was bold because he hated meekness. He was strong because he hated weaklings. Jim's masculinity was a suit he put on every morning, much like his uniform.

He'd wanted to be a cop since his father gave him a plastic badge for his eighth birthday, when he imagined himself wrestling the bad guys to the ground or pointing his gun at them and telling them what to do. By the time he spent one year as a full-time officer in Milwaukee, this desire for authority was compounded with the righteous need to make sure those who thought they could get away with stuff went to jail. No one should get away with anything.

His first years on the force were everything he had imagined, and many things he never could have. There was numbing paperwork, yes, but mostly he rode the night shift—hookers, drug busts, gangs. He took up smoking. The beer he drank in college was replaced more often with whiskey sipped from a shot glass with his buddies after their shifts at 6:00 AM.

Some days were easy, riding around in the car, showing his presence on rough street corners. The bad days were the ones that Jim remembered—the weather, the time, the locations. The days he was called to homes that smelled so bad he stuck cigarette butts up his nose to keep from inhaling the rotting flesh that stuck to carpeting. There were enough bad days in a pay period to make a cop see his job as not worth the cost, and start siphoning money from drug busts into his pocket; enough revulsion in two weeks to let him justify a few missed dope exchanges on the street corners, though he sat in view. He rode past addicts in alleys sticking needles in their arms. Who could possibly keep up?

On the last night of Jim's career in Milwaukee, he was called to a home on a tree-lined street on the north side at eleven o'clock. It was October, but still warm. A neighbor had complained about the music, which Jim could hear even before he shut off his engine. He knocked and rang the doorbell. No answer.

"Jesus Christ," he muttered to himself, and pounded again. "Police!" he yelled. Still nothing.

The door was unlocked. He opened it a crack and peered inside. Smoke and blaring music came at him. Shadows flitted past the door, arms waved in the hazy air. Masked faces appeared, whirling about him as he stepped inside. Jim held up his badge.

"Where is the owner of the house?" he yelled.

The masks laughed at him as they rushed by, Frankenstein, John Wayne, Ronald Reagan. As his eyes adjusted, Jim noticed the people, male and female, were naked. A couple lay together on the couch; three men fondled each other on a blanket on the floor. Vomit crept up Jim's throat.

He turned to step outside and call for backup, but a hand grabbed his shoulder and pulled him around. Marilyn Monroe pouted back at him inches from his face, and her painted fingers rubbed his chest. Another body closed the door behind Jim and pushed up against his backside, hands sliding down his waist. He felt a stirring as Marilyn's fingers brushed down, down, down until they played on his lower abdomen. Then she groped him as she shoved her hips against his, and he grew hard. Marilyn giggled and flipped her hair, turning away from Jim and walking back into the party. That's when Jim saw that Marilyn was a man.

He shoved the man behind him against the front door and put a hand to his throat. He held on longer than he meant to, wanted to squeeze until the guy's head popped. When Jim saw he was about to pass out, he let go and threw him to the floor.

That evening, Jim sat in his car in the parking lot of a shopping center until morning. Then he walked into the station and resigned. He found a job in a small quiet suburb outside of Chicago, knowing his days would be filled with speeding tickets and dead elderly folks. But it was unlikely a middle-class, white-bread suburb had any faggots.

Jim sat in his squad car under a spreading maple tree on a side street in downtown Ackerman. Quiet Ackerman, Illinois.

He knew he should be driving around. Around and around. Seeing nothing and nothing. Waiting for a fast car. Waiting for a stolen stereo—not the whole car, mind you. There were no hijackers in Ackerman. Just young punks who wanted to outfit their shitty cars with high-quality sound.

Three years since he left Milwaukee, and he had yet to solve a real crime. He had yet to arrest a real criminal. And it was killing him. If he wasn't running after murderers, patting down druggies, and handcuffing prostitutes, what was he?

He was a faker—not a real cop, just a loser riding around in a uniform all day. Pretending. And he could tell everyone around him thought the same thing. His wife with her spiky tomato-red hair, her Lee Press-on Nails. Her thighs that had gone from slender to sausages in just a few years. Every time he looked at her, he wanted to punch a wall.

Yesterday a call came over the radio that made him sit upright. Westway Drugs. A possible explosive device in the basement, a bomb threat. He answered the call, turned on his flashing lights and siren, and pulled out of the strip mall parking lot he'd been sitting in on the outskirts of town. A small crowd of people stood on the sidewalk in front of the drugstore when he arrived, the first one. He looked through his windshield at them, his heart pounding with excitement as he grabbed a roll of police tape from the passenger-side floor. The crowd looked to him with wide eyes and followed orders when he opened his car door, yelling, "Everyone to the other side of the street! Now!"

He noticed them briefly as they ran past—a group of junior high schoolers with backpacks hanging off their shoulders; a pregnant lady wearing a floral maternity dress; Andy, still holding a dish-cloth; and a pretty blonde woman he'd never seen before. She made him pause before he shut his car door and turned toward the drug-store, chest heaving.

He'd had some training for this in Milwaukee, though he'd never had to use it. He secured the tape around the building and sidewalk, unrolling it around a tree and his rearview mirror, before going inside. He performed a sweep of the drugstore, then jogged to a door in the far right corner. One stairway led up, one down. Jim ran up. At the top was another door. Unlocked. He opened it and called out. No answer. He entered, and as he searched, to make sure, his eyes rested on a photo of the blonde woman downstairs, and he realized this must be her apartment. He ran past a stack of papers and books on a dining table and into the bedroom. Laundry lay dumped on the bed; lace panties and bras hung from doorknobs and open chest drawers, drying. Outside, he heard more cars arriving, doors slamming.

He ran back down and entered the drug store. A group of three men from the Cook County Sheriff's Office had just arrived, one of them in full protective gear.

The sergeant stepped aside and approached him. "Tom Donnelly," he said. "You just perform a sweep?"

"Upstairs is all clear, sir. Haven't been in the basement yet."

Sergeant Donnelly turned back to the other men. Once they were gone, two in the stairwell, one down into the blackness of the basement, Jim stood in the middle of the store in silence, air rushing in his ears. He didn't think he was supposed to follow them, but he wasn't sure. The people across the street peered in. He wondered if they could see him, standing alone in the store.

After just minutes, the men emerged from the corner door. Jim couldn't tell from their faces what had happened; they were calm, as if completing a chore they'd performed a thousand times. The suited officer took off his headgear as he followed the other officer out.

Sergeant Donnelly paused as he passed Jim. "Nothing. Just a prank." He walked toward the door. "Take care of that crowd outside, will you?" he called over his shoulder.

When Jim stepped outside, the bystanders looked at him, waiting for an explanation, the blonde biting her lip, but he couldn't give it. He tore the caution tape in two, held up a hand toward the crowd, and said, "All clear." Before they could approach him, he got in his car and went home to his small house, his fat wife, and a Hamburger Helper dinner.

As Jim sat in his car under the maple the next day, his eyes caught the blonde exiting the bakery up ahead and across the street. Now, here was the type of woman he should be with. She was lovely. He couldn't find other words. Just lovely. He watched her waist sway as she walked, her calves flex with each step, her skirt ridiculously low, barely above the knee. His friends back home would probably laugh at him had he suggested he was attracted to a girl like her. "Wouldn't you *ever* want to have sex?" they'd ask. He didn't care. He needed someone like her. He already knew what it was like to be with someone he could have sex with any time he wanted.

Julia turned and walked down the street his way, though she didn't see him. When she neared, he pulled his car around in a U-turn and sidled up to her, facing the wrong way on the street. He rolled down his window.

"Hello!" he called.

She turned, startled. "Oh, hello," she said, bending slightly to see inside the car. *My God*, he thought, *her eyes are blue. Blue and perfect*. She threw him a small wave and continued walking.

He crept along with her.

"Would you like a ride?" he asked.

"Oh, thank you, no," she said. "It's only a block." She seemed shy, which turned Jim on.

"You're probably a bit put off by the car," he called, smiling. "Don't worry. I'm allowed. Hop on in." He put the car in park and got out, running around the front to open the passenger door. Julia stopped, though it was several more seconds before she walked to the car and got in. "Jim Clark," he said, tipping his imaginary hat as he held the door open. She smiled. "Julia Parnell."

She sat upright with her hands folded on top of the box of pastries in her lap. Jim nodded toward the box as he drove.

"Whatcha got there?" he asked.

"Some krackling," she said and smiled, a bit sadly Jim thought. "I have a weakness."

Jim nodded, goosebumps dotting his neck at this bit of information, this getting to know her. Lovely Miss Parnell.

She pointed out the front window. "I'm just right up there, at the drug store," she said. "Whatever happened yesterday, anyway?"

Jim had an opportunity here, one he could not pass up. Because to tell the truth, to say, "Nothing was wrong," would be to admit his job was unnecessary.

"Now, there's a story," he said, and he continued past the drug store. Julia inhaled, but the protest stuck in her throat and Jim kept talking. "Drug store got a call, a bomb threat."

"Andy told me; I was at the counter when he got the call. Was it real?"

Jim nodded. "Some nut placed a homemade job in the basement. Don't know if you saw the bomb squad come? I used to be on the squad in Milwaukee. So they sent me down, and I defused it. Deactivated it."

"My goodness, how terrifying."

"Pretty routine, actually." He looked over at her as he turned a corner. "You're not supposed to know this stuff, so keep it on the down low okay?"

Julia nodded and fingered her necklace. "Why would someone place a bomb in the drug store?"

"Who knows," said Jim. "There are a lot of crazy people out there."

"Well, thank you. That sounds weak, but thank you." She waited several seconds before continuing. "I really must get back."

"Help me out, won't you?" he said, leaning his head back against the headrest. "I need company. I mean, can you imagine moments like yesterday and then *this*? Just driving around, waiting for something to happen?"

"I don't envy you," she said, and she contemplated staying, but even Julia had her limits. "I do need to go home, though."

Jim exhaled, long and slow, and Julia could smell cinnamon breath mint. "Alright," he said.

When he pulled up to the curb, he reached his hand across to Julia's shoulder, but she was already stepping out and up. There was a moment when his fingers brushed her shirt but she shrugged away, an involuntary jerk that left him with burning cheeks as he drove off.

Upon entering the drug store, Julia saw Andy at the counter. She waved hello as she walked by.

"Haven't talked to you in a while," he said.

Julia stopped. "I know. I've been so busy with school."

Andy waved her away. "I hear you. Go on, enjoy your muffins."

Julia held up the box. "Krackling. Would you like one? I bought more than I can eat." She walked to the counter and opened the box.

"Don't mind if I do." He reached in.

"Andy, did you find out what happened yesterday?"

He chewed and swallowed. "It was nothing. A prank."

"Oh. I see."

"Why?" Andy nodded toward the front door where he'd just seen Jim drop Julia off. "What'd he say about it?"

But Julia was embarrassed. "Nothing. The same." She smiled. "Please. Have another."

Eleven

Michael carried his *National Geographic* with him everywhere, rolled and slipped into his waistband at his back. He took it to school, placing it in his backpack when he had to sit at his desk and retrieving it for recess, when he could sit under his tree and read and feel at home.

At Tina's house for dinner, he took the magazine out of his waistband and placed it on the kitchen table before he sat down.

"What you got there?" asked Jim Clark as he passed a plate of grilled hamburgers. Jim often cooked dinners on the grill, which he placed on the driveway in view of the rest of the block instead of the back patio where most people kept theirs.

"It's a *National Geographic* about wolves," said Michael.

"Michael loves wolves," said Tina.

"We used to watch them back home all the time. There was a den with seven wolves and my dad knew all about them, each one. He took me with him."

"Uh huh." Jim nodded toward the magazine. "You always carry that around?"

Michael nodded, and Jim smirked, glancing at his wife, who responded dutifully with raised eyebrows. She grabbed her hamburger with two hands, fingers taut because of her wet pink nails. While chewing her food, she shoved it to one side of her cheek and said, "Might want to keep it under your chair if it's so valuable so it doesn't get greasy."

Michael did as he was told and then readied his hamburger with ketchup and mayonnaise. He started to cut it in half, but the plastic knife broke part way through.

"I'll get you another," said Cassie, rising. She handed him a blue knife from the multi-colored pack on the counter. "Don't feel like doing dishes tonight."

Michael looked at a vase of colored paper flowers in the center of the table.

"Those are pretty," he said.

Cassie brightened. "Thanks, sweetie." She looked at Jim as she continued. "Those were my first gift from Jim. He knew I loved rainbows, and he couldn't find any real rainbow flowers, so he brought me those."

"I knew there weren't any real rainbow flowers, Cassie. I was just going to try to find the colors of the rainbow. I saw those instead."

"I know."

"I painted my mom that rainbow in kindergarten," said Tina, pointing to a framed picture on the wall behind Cassie.

Cassie rose and took the picture down. "This rainbow is my absolute favorite," she said, holding the outside of the frame with her palms so she didn't smudge the glass, then turned it toward Michael. "Can you believe she was only five when she made this?"

Michael smiled.

"I met that new teacher of yours yesterday, Mike," said Jim. "We got a call to her building. You know, she lives above Westway Drugs."

"What happened?" asked Cassie.

Jim ignored his wife. "She seems real nice. Do you like her?"

"Yeah."

"She's real pretty, huh? I bet your other teachers don't look like her."

Cassie leaned the picture against the wall and grabbed the bottle of Zinfandel on the table to refill her glass. Jim rose from the table and took a can of beer from the refrigerator.

"She's not prettier than Mom, is she Dad?" asked Tina.

He popped open the beer and took a sip. "No, honey, of course not. No one's prettier than your mother."

As he walked back to the table with his head tilted back drinking, some drops spilled onto the floor, his boot stepping on them and tracking the beer across the tile.

"Daddy, can you do whistles?" asked Tina.

Michael watched Jim as he took another drink of beer and licked his lips. He readied himself as the children waited and finally let out a long, loud burp.

Tina laughed and Michael threw a hand to his mouth.

"Daddy!" said Tina.

"Okay, okay. Let me try again." He repeated the process of drinking his beer and licking his lips, then placed his thumb and index finger to his mouth and blew. A piercing whistle came out, three notes strung together—high-low-high.

"Do a chickadee!" Tina said, and her father acquiesced, as well as to the subsequent requests for a robin, cardinal, and mourning dove.

"Isn't that cool?" Tina asked Michael, and he nodded. This small sound of the natural world made him happy.

But Jim had grown tired of whistling.

"Who wants to hear some cop stories?" he asked, leaning back in his chair and running a hand through his black hair.

"I do!" said Michael, though Tina slumped her shoulders and Cassie rose from the table to throw the plates away. Then she walked down the hall to her bedroom.

"What do you wanna know?" asked Jim. "Good guys? Bad buys? Drug busts?"

"Bad guys," said Michael.

"Do you want to know about the baddest guy ever, the worst one I ever put away?"

Michael nodded eagerly.

Jim settled back in his chair. "It was four in the afternoon, July 22, 1978. We got an APB—do you know what that is, Mike?"

Michael shook his head.

"That's an All Points Bulletin. A call from the station to be on the lookout for a suspect."

"What suspect?" asked Michael.

"Well, some black kids at a park witnessed a man commit a horrible crime."

Michael's eyes widened. "What crime?"

"Patience, Mike. So, I headed to the spot where the guy was last seen, an apartment building overlooking the same park. I spoke with the residents. Asked around. Did some investigating. Turns out the guy had a girlfriend who lived in the building. His own place was a few blocks away. So I headed there." He paused to take a drink of beer.

"Was he there?" asked Michael.

"Yep. Smoking dope on his couch. Tried to run away, but I arrested the son of a bitch right then and there."

"What did he do?"

Jim took another drink and landed his beer can on the table with a crack. "He dropped his girlfriend's kid out a tenth-story window for spilling ketchup on the couch."

Michael swallowed. He had never heard of something like this before. He hadn't known it existed. The image pounded into his brain, made a space for itself there quickly and without pause in a way that reminded him too much of his father's death, and he grew angry.

"Okay, Michael," called Cassie from her bedroom. "Time to go home."

Tina rose to walk Michael across the street because she sensed there might be an argument between her parents. She often left whenever this happened, walking around the block a few times in dusk or darkness. When she returned, she knew the fight would be over and shoved aside or she would have to sit with her mother awhile.

This night, she had to sit with her mother, but not for too long.

Cassie had had too much Zinfandel, so she was tired. They sat in Cassie's bed together, cross-legged.

"Your father needs to stop telling those stories," said Cassie. But that just upset Tina because her mother had never asked him to stop.

Cassie waved her away. "He won't listen to me. He thinks I'm a nag." She pulled a cigarette out of her pack and grabbed a lighter from the bedside table. "We should have Miss Parnell tell him." She smiled sideways at her daughter.

"Are you jealous of her?" asked Tina.

Cassie lit the cigarette and exhaled toward the ceiling. "They think she's gay, you know. Lezbo. A woman at the salon has a sister from somewhere around where she used to live. Might have even lived with a woman." Cassie chuckled a smoky rasp. "If it's true, your father's going to make a fool of himself."

She asked Tina to stay until she fell asleep, and it was just a few minutes before she started snoring. Then Tina snuck out and went to her own room.

When Michael returned from school the next day, he sat in his kitchen eating an apple, reminded how quiet his home was now, an empty space waiting for him every afternoon. Even meals with his mother were quieter, with no third person to overtake the pockets of silence punctuated by clanking silverware. Though Tina's house often gave him a feeling like homesickness, it was something to do.

He left a note on the counter for his mother and jogged across the street.

"Want to play a game of ball tag?" he asked when Tina answered the door. "We should be able to play with only two people."

"That's for babies," she replied through the screen door.

"Oh." He turned to go.

"Twist my arm," she said and rolled her eyes. "Let's stay here.

I have a better backyard." She was wearing a shirt with a rainbow painted across the front and down both arms. When she held the door open, the rainbow got wings. "I have to find the ball in the basement."

Inside, Jim sat in the kitchen drinking a beer. Three crushed cans lay on the table, though it was only four o'clock.

Tina turned to Michael. "Stay here."

Jim stood up and walked to the refrigerator. "Want some Cokes?"

"Sure," said Michael. Jim opened two bottles and handed them over. Then he walked back to the kitchen table and sat down, staring at his beer, while Michael stood in the middle of the kitchen holding the pop.

"I had to leave work early today," said Jim. "Back's killing me. It's not easy sitting in a car all day with a sore back."

Michael did not know what was called for, so he just said, "Sorry." They remained in silence for a minute while Michael wondered what kinds of things Jim had seen in Ackerman, but he didn't want to know. Tina finally came up from the basement and tossed a rubber ball to Michael, who caught it between his two fists of Coke, making Tina laugh. Once outside, they put their feet together and Tina bent down, pointing from toe to toe as she recited the familiar counting-out rhyme. It was the same one Michael and his friends used back in Minnesota, and this made him happy.

"My mother and your mother were washing the clothes. My mother punched your mother right in the nose. What color was the blood?"

"Green," said Michael.

"G-R-E-E-N." She landed on her own foot. "I'm out. You're it."

Michael chased Tina through the yard, behind the shed, and around to the front. She was quite fast, which surprised Michael. He'd never had a hard time with anything physical and in Minnesota was often picked as a pinch runner even when he was already in the game.

She kept racing around back and forth like she was dodging

bullets, and he couldn't get a good angle. But when Tina ran behind the privacy fence separating her house from the neighbor's, Michael jumped onto the roof of the car in her driveway and threw the ball down at her, hitting the top of her head.

"Ow!" yelled Tina, grabbing her head, her ponytail askew. "That's not fair!" She ran through her front door, leaving Michael alone and unsure what to do. He was about to walk home when Jim came out with Tina.

"What were you thinking, Mike?" Jim yelled. "You think you can roughhouse with a girl?" He continued walking toward Michael.

"Daddy," said Tina, and she grabbed his hand.

"Do you?" yelled Jim.

Michael's eyes welled. He dropped the ball and left, embarrassed and confused. He'd never been yelled at by an adult before.

When he walked in the door, his mother was home.

"Hello, honey. Come sit by me." She patted the couch where she was lying. The brown and orange afghan she'd crocheted when Michael was a baby, when his father was alive, was draped across her.

"Is it okay with you if we have sandwiches tonight?" she asked. "I've been around food all day. I'm not in the mood to cook it."

Michael nodded.

"How was Tina's?"

"Fine."

Anne lifted her head to watch her son. She could see that something was off, had been since John's death, of course. She wished she could make it all better, kiss it away. But she didn't need to know the details of Michael's life, she told herself. There were dark spots and bright spots, and side-by-side they just had to make it through this darkness. Through it or around it, she didn't know, but she would not let the darkness overtake them, would not let the pain into the room with them. That was her job.

"Things will get better," she said. "They always do. Wait and see."

Michael did not want to wait. He was used to doing things, to leading his friends through baseball games, sledding competitions, and school. He was used to people liking him, and he'd always assumed he deserved their respect because he was likable, a good person. No one had ever said a thing about him being adopted or having AIDS or throwing a ball too hard. There were too many rules in this new world that he didn't understand, and he ached—deeply ached—to return to his real home. Sometimes when he slept, he was really there and could smell the pines. Those were his favorite moments of the day.

"Have you made any more friends at school?" his mother asked.

"A few," he lied, angry with his mother for forcing out his shame.

She smiled and laid her head back on the pillow.

In his room, he took his *National Geographic* out of his pocket and tried to read, to calm himself. But his tears blurred the page, and he watched a large drop fall down onto the ear of a gray wolf and spread as the paper absorbed it. Each one he watched fall and expand until the paper was damp and warped, the wolf pitted. And then, as Michael sat, the paper dried, harder than it was before.

The next morning, Tina showed up at Michael's house to walk to school.

"He scares me, too, sometimes," she said. "But he won't do anything. He just gets like that when he has too much beer."

Tina told Michael she would have to stay inside at recess that day. No sitting by the fence. She needed to go to the library for tutoring in reading because she hated books and did not care what the meanings were behind the words. "Why not just *say* what you mean, for Christ sake?" she asked. Sometimes Michael thought Tina sounded a lot older than she was.

Michael sat under the tree and read his *National Geographic*, happy to be alone. He didn't feel like talking today, or pretending. He flipped through the pictures as he had a hundred times. The fur, the snouts, the eyes became three-dimensional, and Michael could step inside, away from the playground.

He suddenly realized four boys were standing in front of him, including Jason and Peter.

"Where's your friend?" asked Jason.

"Inside," said Michael.

"What's that?"

"A magazine, Sherlock."

The boys around Jason chuckled. Jason's eyes burned on Michael, but Michael didn't flinch.

"Uh, yeah, thanks retard," said Jason. "I know it's a magazine. Why are you always reading it?"

"Shouldn't you leave? You might get AIDS."

But Jason ignored him and smiled. "Can I see?" he asked, holding out his hand.

Michael hesitated. He didn't want to hand it over, but he wanted to keep them happy so they would go away. He gave Jason the magazine.

Jason snatched it and thumbed through the pages. "Boring," he said, and threw the magazine up in the air to Peter, who caught only two of the pages on its way down. The pages tore from the binding, prompting another boy to pick the magazine up and tear more, then throw it to the next boy. The pages began to scatter, to slide across the field on the wind. Michael watched just one page as it flew, the cover of the wolf, watched as it rolled away and caught on the branch of a bush. When the boys dashed, Michael stood and walked over to the bush. He folded the cover carefully and slid it in his pocket, then returned to the tree.

He rested back against the tree trunk and felt it's bark push against his skin. He breathed the air that rustled the tree leaves and made them whisper down to him. Shushing him, shushing him. He drew his knees to his chest and closed his eyes, listening. The sound wrapped around him, the trunk held him, and he fell asleep.

He did not know how long he slept or what woke him, but

when he looked up, recess was over. Miss Parnell walked across the field. Her skirt swayed with her hair, and she looked down at her crossed arms, glancing up only every few steps. When she reached Michael, she sat down partway around the trunk and rested against it, extending her legs and crossing them at the ankle.

"I won't go back in," said Michael, hugging his knees.

"You have to."

"It's not fair."

"I know. Still, it's there to do."

"Do you even know what they did?"

Julia looked at the pages scattered across the field. "Yes," she said. "Jason will have a detention."

"Why can't you make them stop?"

"I don't know, Michael. I don't know. I've talked with the principal, I've talked with their parents. We have no school policy that says this is anything other than mischief, regular schoolyard antics. Jason claimed the soccer ball was an accident. But, listen to me." She shifted to her side to face Michael. "They're wrong. The school is wrong."

He wouldn't look at her. "So what?"

"It matters that you know. That you don't think you deserve this. Or that you don't think you should feel as upset as you do. They're being awful."

"I hate it here." He began to cry and placed his forehead on his knees.

"Have you talked to your mother?"

He sniffled and wiped a cheek. "A little." He didn't want to lie but did not want to have to explain why he hadn't told her, the shame he felt, because saying it out loud might make it true. He didn't yet know that if he just released it, shared it with someone else, it would be diminished, somehow get smaller as it went out into the world.

"Michael, people are naturally scared of new things, and to these kids, adoption is new. *You're* new."

"I think some people are just mean."

Julia sighed. "You're probably right. But if they're just mean, then it has nothing to do with you." She rose and brushed off her skirt. "You know, I live right next to the ice cream shop. Would you like to get some after school?"

Michael nodded.

She held out her hand. "Let's go in now. We'll call your mother from the office and let her know."

Michael walked down the street toward Baskin-Robbins with Miss Parnell and watched as people noticed her. Not only men but women, too, looked as they passed. One woman stopped them and asked Miss Parnell where she got her dress, she hadn't seen a shirt dress with an A-line anywhere and simply loved them. Miss Parnell responded that she'd bought it in Iowa, or Kansas, or somewhere else that Michael didn't hear because he was looking at her thinking, yes, she looked like the moms in old children's books with the perfect nose and lips and little waist and waved hair.

Then Michael realized they were talking about him. Miss Parnell had put a hand on his shoulder and said, "No, I don't have children. This is my student, Michael. I'm taking him out for ice cream."

"Well, how nice," said the woman, "to take the time after school."

The two sat on stools in the ice cream shop, licking their cones.

"I'm boring, I guess," said Julia. "I've loved vanilla since I was a girl."

"Did you grow up here?" asked Michael.

"No, I grew up in Kansas."

"Did you live on a farm?"

"No, in a town kind of like this."

"Why did you come here?"

"For my job."

"Are we your first class?" asked Michael.

"Yes. I was going to teach at a school in Iowa, but I left." She didn't know why she included that.

"Why?"

Julia hesitated. "Remember when you said today you thought

some people were just mean?" Michael nodded. "Well, I ran into a few of those people in Iowa." She realized she was constructing something the way she wanted it to be, not the way it was.

"Why didn't they like you?"

"For the same reason some of those kids made fun of you."

"You're adopted?"

"No, but they thought I was different, and some people don't like different."

"I think we should make *those* people go," said Michael.

Julia smiled. "Me, too."

Twelve

Anne's hands were used to flipping eggs in a skillet, grasping a cow's udder, scrubbing little toes in the bathtub. She would have to create new memories for her hands so they were as quick and deft as that. In the first week of her job, Anne spilled soda at the waitress station, and it dripped into the ice bin so that all the ice had to be removed scoopful by scoopful and hauled away in buckets so new ice could be hauled back in. And she hadn't thought to warn a man standing at the bar that she was walking behind him with a tray full of food, so when he turned around and his shoulder hit the tray, plates, fries, lettuce, and buns scattered across the floor. At one point she spilled water—thank goodness, water—on the lap of a businessman dining with a client.

But, by the end of her first month at Murphy's, she knew what Glenfiddich and Glenlivet were and could figure out the fastest way to complete six tasks in seconds. There were only so many things involved in taking care of tables, and she mastered them all. She simply took orders and gave people what they wanted. Pick up Patio Table 5's drink order; on the way out the door, grab two menus for Table 3; drop off the menus with a friendly "I'll be right with you" and deliver Table 5's drinks, placing their dirty glasses on the now-empty tray; on the way back to Table 3, ask Table 4 how their food is and pick up any empty dishes—they'll probably ask for extra silverware or napkins, so hand them the extras you've thoughtfully stored in your apron pocket; take Table 3's drink order and let them know the soup of the day before heading back inside to drop off your dirty dishes—glasses to the bar and plates in the bin for the busboys to take downstairs; hand Table 3's drink order to the bartender and prepare any nonalcoholic beverages. Et cetera.

She liked the frankness of it; there was no room for interpretation, no pressure to create or solve—except in how to best multitask, but for Anne that was easy. She began to look at her job, if not her coworkers, as a respite where there was an answer for everything. Here, unlike at home, she could solve a problem and put it behind her. Here, she did not think about John; her mind stayed sharp and focused and didn't melt into sorrow as it so often did at home.

And with every pour, every step, every plate placed down, she knew she was providing for Michael, as John always had. She wasn't providing a lot—her first month, she had $13.07 left over after paying for rent, groceries, a new shirt for Michael, and an oil change on her truck. But as she moved around the restaurant, shifting, turning, lifting, placing, she felt active. She was *doing*. And while part of her knew there was more to her job as a mother, all she could focus on right now was figuring out how to provide.

Her focus was so strong, she pushed past her insecurity and discomfort every time she opened the tavern doors and faced her coworkers. They were hard. *It takes a certain kind of person to work at a bar*, Anne thought. They were not like her. Their language was hard, their mascara, their hair. Waitresses like Molly, who was sweet and simple, came only during summer break. Once school started, the sweet and simples drifted off and the adamantine remained, like the heavy oak beams of the tavern. People like Nancy did not suffer fools—not the intellectually foolish but the emotionally foolish. If one was too nice or too sensitive, one did not last among the gum cracking and hard consonants of the waitresses at Murphy's. Lucky for Anne, she was from Norwegian-farmer stock. She was not like these waitresses, but she knew how to set up a wall as thick as theirs. Still, every time she arrived at work, she felt homesick. These people reminded her she was not in Minnesota, on her farm, with John. And she hated them for it.

Anne opened the large wooden door to Murphy's on a Wednesday morning and walked through last night's air, putrid with stale smoke and beer. She stuffed her purse into the cubby and wrapped her black cloth apron around her waist, then tied her hair back into a low ponytail. When she finished, she ran her hands along the front of her to smooth and ready herself for the day, stopping to scrape dried ketchup off her apron with a bare, clipped nail.

"Morning," said Kevin, behind her.

Anne turned and smiled. "You're here." She still wasn't used to the sight of him without those huge glasses; he'd started wearing contact lenses several years ago. His eyes looked a much deeper brown. Just like Michael's.

"Got back last night," he said.

She often seemed close to her brother, working within the walls of his own restaurant, and yet she rarely saw him. He traveled so much for business she hadn't even had him over to their new house, and she had no idea where he lived exactly. He had no wife, no children, so there were no extended family dinners or cousin play dates to consider. She often thought she might as well still be living in Minnesota for as much as she saw him.

"I've been meaning to ask you over for dinner," she said. "You've barely had a chance to see Michael."

"How's he like school?"

"Alright, I think."

"Can't be easy for him right now."

"Easy, no. But you'd be surprised what kids can handle." She immediately regretted what seemed a reference to his lack of children, or to his own childhood. He just shrugged and turned toward the stairs.

"I'll be in the office," he said over his shoulder. Her heart ached a bit.

She watched Chip wipe down the bar first with a damp cloth and then with oil. She knew more than to sit on a barstool and possibly smudge his work before customers came in. They were the only ones allowed to touch the bar and use the ashtrays, though Anne thought sometimes Chip looked disappointed when even they sat down. The wall behind Chip was covered with a mirror, fronted by shelves of liquor. A neon sign above the cash register advertised Pabst Blue Ribbon.

The bar shone almost as bright as Chip's teeth. Anne had wondered often if he was a model. He was certainly good looking enough. She should just ask him, but that might be prying. Plus, his ego would probably lead him to think she was interested in him. The thought made Anne chuckle.

"What?" asked Chip.

"Nothing." Anne leaned against the waitress station. "Any missing today?"

"Four bucks," said Chip. He stopped wiping. "I just can't figure it out. It's enough for me to notice, but not enough to possibly be worth it. Kevin needs to get on this A-sap." Chip was always saying that—"A-sap"—as a word and not an acronym: "I need ice, A-sap. Get me a side of pickles, A-sap." It bothered Anne, but who was she to judge? Every time she said "Oh, fly," when she forgot a side of mayo or an extra slice of onion, Nancy smirked.

"Who's outside today?" called Nancy as she came through the door, holding a cigarette. "Just started raining."

Anne knew what that meant. One of them would be let go for the day. It was one thing when it rained or was slow during the summer—the college kids always wanted to be let off early, and when they saw storm clouds, they cheered. But for Anne and the other waitresses who worked to live, rain was not welcome.

"Up to you two," said Chip.

Nancy crushed out her cigarette in one of the ashtrays on the bar.

"Goddamn it," he said, taking it and dumping it in the slop bucket. He wiped the ashtray clean.

Nancy ignored him. "I went home last time," she said to Anne, and began taking down chairs.

As she drove through the rain, Anne felt a small pinpoint of pressure in her chest. Her meager leftovers from last month were the result of working every shift she was assigned, plus often staying the extra hour and a half until the dinner shift arrived. She could not afford any lost hours. The pressure increased, and she made a conscious effort to inhale deeply, but she could not breathe deep enough for relief. The air was heavy, humid from the rain. She stopped the truck at a red light and tried again for a deep breath. She had to take care of Michael; she couldn't fail at that. She held onto the steering wheel and inhaled, smelling car exhaust and her own damp coat. The light turned green, but she was looking at the windshield, watching the drops hit the glass and spread downward into a sheet of water. A car honked. She turned the truck around.

When she entered the office, Kevin was hunched over a calculator on his desk. He looked up over his reading glasses. *My God*, thought Anne, *my little brother has reading glasses.*

"Nancy told me you went home," he said.

Anne sat down in a chair facing his desk. "I need another shift."

He nodded. "What are you thinking?"

"If I bring Michael with me for dinner, I could work a Friday or Saturday night and just send him home for bed. It's not too far."

Kevin blinked several times. "The thing is, Anne, the other waitresses have been here so long, and those shifts are valuable. I can't bump one of them."

"Right, of course. I didn't think of that."

"What about Saturday afternoon?"

"I hate to leave Michael alone all day."

"I'm gone so much on weekends, otherwise I'd—"

Anne shook her head. "Oh, no. I understand. You've got your own worries."

"Is there anyone? A neighbor?"

"I'll take Saturdays," said Anne. "And I'll figure out the rest."

That afternoon, she walked down the wet street to the school to pick up Michael. She asked him to wait in the hallway while she talked to Miss Parnell.

"I'm not sure whether you know our situation," she said, holding tight to the purse strap on her shoulder as she stood in front of Miss Parnell's desk. "Michael's father—"

Julia nodded. "I do," she said quietly.

"I'm working, but it's not quite enough. I need to add Saturdays, and I was thinking maybe once in a while you could take Michael for ice cream again or to the show. I would pay, of course." Julia sat listening, and Anne's hands turned clammy, grasping the purse strap. "I don't know anyone else and I just, I need help. Sometimes I feel like if I blink I might lose my balance and everything will fall apart."

"Of course I'll help," said Julia. "I'm glad I can. Michael's a sweet boy."

Anne smiled. "Yes."

"You know, he's having a hard time with some of the other boys."

Anne flinched. "Of course. It's no wonder with the move and the new school and his father . . ."

Julia saw the devastation in Anne's eyes, the pleading that said, "Please. I can't hold any more."

And so she said only, "Let's plan on every Saturday, unless I hear from you."

When Anne came out, Michael stood in the hallway looking up at the wall, where photos and biographies of the students in his class were posted.

"Jason has three brothers and a sister," he said.

"Who's Jason? Your friend?"

"No." He started walking down the hallway, and Anne followed.

"I had to pick up another shift," she said. "Saturdays."

"Ok."

"You'll spend the afternoons with Miss Parnell. That will be nice, won't it?"

"Ok."

"Michael, I'm sorry. I'm just not making enough."

"It's fine, Mom. I like Miss Parnell."

"I know you do." She exhaled. "Much to my relief." She placed a hand on Michael's shoulder as they continued on down the hallway.

Anne had asked Kevin for dinner that night. When she answered the door, he stood on the doorstep with a baked ham.

"Oh," said Anne, "I already have lasagna in the oven."

"Of course, no. This is just—just for whenever." He offered the ham over the threshold to Anne, then followed her to the kitchen, where she placed the ham on the table. Kevin stood with his coat on.

"Here, let me take that," said Anne. "Would you like a drink?"

"Thanks, no. I don't drink anymore."

"Oh?" she asked over her shoulder as she placed the coat on a hook by the kitchen door to the backyard.

"I see too much of it now. It lost its appeal."

"Kevin the teetotaler, owner of a bar."

"Not sure I'd go that far. Just don't care for it myself."

"Yes. I was only joking."

Kevin looked around. "So this is the new house. Not the same as the farm, I guess."

Anne eyed the brown linoleum, the olive green appliances. The kitchen decor had been trendy ten years ago, lacked the staying power of a white farmhouse sink and wood floors. "No. Not much is the same now. Everything's changed."

"Except you and Michael," he offered.

Anne nodded. She allowed herself to wonder briefly whether it was true—were she and Michael the same? She didn't think they could be, not possibly, but she couldn't pull herself back far enough from their new lives to see. She was living not day by day, but minute by minute. There was an ache in her chest, a twisting in her stomach, feelings that had become part of her life. She didn't know if she was doing worse or better than she should be. She never could have imagined what it felt like to lose a husband, could never have imagined how to survive each moment, every reminder—the steering wheel he used to guide lightly with thumb and forefinger, the cereal he ate with a fork, her own fingers he once held. And Michael.

And now, with no choice but to get through it, finding that she was. It sometimes surprised her that she was still alive, that she was doing, moment by moment, what she'd never imagined. That while her body carried itself differently, mostly aching, sometimes numb, she was proceeding through this new life, however narrowly.

"We're getting through," she said. "Here, let me go get him."

They sat down to eat.

"This is nice," said Anne. "It's been awhile since there were three of us at the table." As soon as she spoke, she was sorry for the words, sorry to have brought John into the room.

"How is school?" asked Kevin.

Michael looked up from his plate and, it seemed to Anne, forced a smile. "Good!" he said, a little too brightly. Anne saw something behind his eyes and knew she should ask him about the other boys Miss Parnell had mentioned.

"He has a wonderful teacher," she said instead.

Kevin nodded. "That always helps."

The kitchen was quiet except for the sounds of their eating.

"I bet you miss Minnesota," Kevin said after a few moments. *No, Kevin*, thought Anne. She glanced at her son.

But Michael looked relieved. "Uh huh. I miss it a lot. I can't wait to go back."

"Oh? Are you going to visit?"

Michael looked at his mother. "Sometime. Right?"

"Oh, I'm sure we'll plan something." She cut her lasagna.

"My best friend Pike's back there. He said I can stay with them.

Maybe I can go over winter break. His dad might take us hiking in the woods." He didn't tell them that if he got back there, he wasn't going to leave. He was going to live with Pike's family. "My dad used to take me."

"I do remember he had a fondness for the woods," said Kevin. "I sometimes miss Minnesota. When I was a boy, I'd head out to the lakes early on a summer morning with my fishing pole. I'd pack a lunch and be gone all day. I don't know if I could sit still that long anymore."

"Can I go fishing with you?" asked Michael. "You could take me Saturday when Mom's at work."

Kevin had been lost in his memory, but now he looked at Michael and then down at his plate. "Oh, I don't know. I'm usually out of town every weekend. But maybe. Maybe sometime."

After dinner, Michael went off to finish his homework and Anne stayed at the table with her brother.

"When I called you after John died . . . I didn't mean for you to have to take care of us. I didn't mean for us to invade your life here. If I'd had other options . . ."

"Of course, Anne. I would hope you'd call me rather than sit alone up there trying to scrape together a living."

"That's what I'm doing here." She tried to laugh.

"You're not invading my life. It's your life too now, anyway."

"Sometimes I think I should have stayed. For Michael."

"What would you have done? John hadn't even planted yet. There would have been no crop to cash in."

"Baked. Canned. Started a business. Used my degree. I made the decision so fast."

"You were going to have a baby."

"Yes."

Kevin rose from the table with his plate—too soon, and she felt a twinge of anger at him for leaving her alone, even just at the table, with her memories. Anger that he seemed so uninterested in her pain, in everything.

"Will you take Michael fishing?" she asked, but there was a tone to her voice, a dare.

"I don't know where we'd go around here."

"You can find someplace."

"Sure, sometime."

"When?"

"I don't know, Anne." He rinsed his plate under the faucet.

"Did you even like John?"

"Of course. Who didn't?"

"I always imagined that you and whatever husband I had would be best friends, like we used to be." It was an accusation.

He faced her and leaned back against the sink, arms crossed against his chest, but his eyes had no fight in them. "I was too far away."

She didn't want to fight, either. It didn't suit her. She tried, instead, to lighten the conversation. "What about you? Is there a woman I can be best friends with?" Her eyes twinkled.

But Kevin just frowned and shook his head. "No."

When Miss Parnell announced recess the next day, Michael remained at his desk and watched the children line up at the doorway. Miss Parnell led them outside, where other teachers were waiting to supervise the playground.

"No recess today?" she asked when she returned.

Michael shook his head.

"You know, I could use your help." She waved a hand over her desk. "I have all these papers to grade, and those bookshelves are incredibly out of order. They need to be alphabetized. Would you mind?"

"Sure." He set to work as Miss Parnell flipped through the papers on her desk.

He saw *To Kill a Mockingbird* and remembered it was his father's favorite book. Whenever Michael had to earn reading points at school, his father sat with him on the couch and read aloud from his worn copy. *Funny*, he thought. Jem and Scout didn't have a mother and he didn't have a father anymore. But that did not feel right. He did still have a father; he felt it was so.

"Do you think someone can have a father even if he can't talk to him?" he asked.

Miss Parnell smiled, and knew the significance of the question. "I do."

"Even if he's not there to make rules or help with homework?"

"Even so."

"But what about later? When," Michael searched for the words, "when I get older and new stuff happens, stuff I never did with him?"

"You're here, aren't you? That's new. And you're doing okay."

"I guess."

"His influence will remain, Michael. He taught you all that he needed to teach you."

But Michael was not comforted.

"Your mother will remind you," she said.

"What if she doesn't know?"

"She knew your father for a long time. She'll know. Why don't you write down everything you remember? Even if it doesn't seem significant. Then you'll always have it."

He considered the idea. He thought about his father all the time, mostly memories, but also sometimes his father just showed up alongside him. The only way he would be able to know later what was a real memory was the place—if he remembered his father here, in Ackerman, he would know it was not real. But maybe he should write down those times anyway, while his father was still so fresh in his mind he knew exactly what he might say or how he might look.

"I could make a book," he said.

"That's a wonderful idea." Miss Parnell opened a desk drawer. "I have just the thing," she said, pulling out a journal. Then, "I have something else for you. A present. I was going to wait until Saturday." She held out a *National Geographic* with a wolf on the cover, the same issue the boys had torn.

Michael jumped toward it and grabbed it with both hands. "How did you find it? It's two months old."

"We teachers are resourceful."

Michael remembered himself and looked up from the magazine. "Thank you," he said, and blushed, hugging it to his chest.

"You are most welcome."

"We used to go out in the woods and watch them. Well, one time we did. I could put it in my book."

"You had better. That's not something to forget."

"He let me come along to search for traps once, too. Even though my mother didn't like it. He thought I was old enough. And we found a wolf. My father had to shoot it. So it wouldn't suffer."

Michael walked back to the bookshelf with his magazine and sat on the floor.

"Are you married?" he asked after a few moments and then was visibly embarrassed.

"It's alright," said Julia. "No, I'm not."

"Do you want to be?"

"I'm not really sure."

"A girl back home once told me girls have to be skinny when they get married," said Michael. "They have to go on diets. Her sister was married."

"Well, she was wrong. You don't have to be skinny to get married. You just have to find someone you love and who loves you." Of course, that wasn't quite true, either. She returned to grading.

"You haven't yet?" asked Michael.

"Haven't what?"

"Found someone you love?"

"No." The lie came easily. "I haven't."

"The girl was stupid, anyway," said Michael. "She wore tutus to school, and leg warmers. She worked out during recess."

"No one your age should work out. Girls, particularly."

"Why?"

"They should just focus on being healthy. Girls are hard enough on themselves as it is. About their physical appearance, anyway."

Michael was interested. He'd never had a conversation like this before. Certainly not with his mother. "Why?" he asked.

"I don't know. Magazines are full of skinny women. Maybe it's in our blood. Maybe we learn it from our mothers and the cycle just keeps going and going."

"Are you hard on yourself?"

Julia sighed. "I suppose I am. I worry how I look in almost everything I wear. I hate my arms."

Michael crinkled his nose. "Your arms?"

"Yes. They're flabby."

"Oh."

"But see, there, I just did it. Oh, Michael," she sighed. "Don't let the world ruin you. Do you like yourself?" She was speaking of his physical self, but he didn't know that.

He nodded. He thought he did. He always had, up until now.

"Good! Always remember that, how you felt about yourself when you were nine. Don't one day decide not to like some part of you because you think it's not good enough, because someone told you it's not good enough." It was so easy to tell others. "When you're older, all kinds of messy things will get in the way of clear thinking. So remind yourself that when you were younger and smarter, you liked yourself."

Except Michael was thinking how a lot of kids here didn't like him, and he had to wonder whether they had a point.

On a Friday in early October, Michael sat on the classroom floor after school cutting letters from red construction paper for a sign on the wall that would read, "Reading Corner." Miss Parnell had brought in three beanbag chairs and a little braided rug to make a cozy spot.

In addition to their Saturdays together, Michael had been often staying inside at recess or after school if Miss Parnell had work for him to do, and she usually did. He told Tina he was getting tutored in the library and couldn't walk home with her anymore, but one day she peeked in and he wasn't there. So she continued to wait for him outside the school every afternoon. Once in a while, he showed up.

"We can do whatever you like tomorrow," Julia said to Michael from her desk. "I'm at your disposal."

Michael tried to think of something that would remind him of home. "I know," he said. "Horses!"

"Horses?"

"At the racetrack. We used to go every summer in Minnesota."

The next day, Anne dropped off Michael in front of the drugstore, where Julia was waiting on the sidewalk. Anne leaned over to the passenger window to hand Julia money and told her, "If I were you, I'd let Michael make your bets. He wins every time."

"I'll take that advice. I've never been to a racetrack before. Have a good day at work."

Anne watched her son leave with Julia. Saturday used to be family day. If it was summer, she and John watched Michael's baseball games, or they all rode to town together for a movie if it was hot. Last year at this time, early fall, they were nearing the end of harvest. Anne imagined Michael sitting with John in the tractor, receiving one of the many lessons on safety and respect for farm equipment. She remembered picking raspberries from the large bushes scattered along the side of their yard, and could see them, father and son, side-by-side, Michael's shoulder touching John's arm just above the elbow.

She watched Michael turn the corner with Julia, a woman she liked but barely knew, a woman she hadn't known existed a year ago. This is just how it is now, she told herself.

The grandstand at Ackerman Park gleamed in the October sun. Except for the roof and the seats, which were green, the entire structure was white. A large, circular bed of red flowers, with a giant white "A" in the middle, greeted them as they walked up the incline from the parking lot, among a stream of people. It was the last racing weekend of the season.

"I feel like I should be wearing a giant hat," said Julia.

"Why?" asked Michael.

"That's just what women typically wear to the races. Mostly in the South."

"Oh. Well, I don't think they do that here."

"No, this is decidedly not the South."

"Does everyone where you come from always wear dresses and skirts?"

"I suppose we do dress up more back home."

"My mom says you look classic."

"Well, that is the best compliment I could ask for."

Julia paid for their tickets, and they walked through the ground floor, up the staircase, and out into the grandstand. The oval outer track, encircled by a white wooden fence, was covered in soft, fresh brown dirt. On the far side, opposite the grandstand, a long row of willows bordered the park.

"It's just beautiful," said Julia.

The place bustled. Men in suits reclined as they read the racing programs, toddlers zigzagged among the knees walking up and down the grandstand steps, young teenagers skittered about like schools of bullhead minnows. Julia steered Michael away from a group of men smoking cigars, chest hair pushing out of their silk button-down shirts. They found space on a bench a few rows up from the track, near a woman breastfeeding her child, and studied their programs before the first race.

"What does *Allegra* mean?" asked Michael.

"Fast," said Julia.

"What does *Paint The Town Red* mean?"

"That means having fun. Like, I'm going to paint the town red."

"Why?"

"I don't really know."

"Who is *Jack Daniels*?"

"That's the name of a brand of liquor."

"What about *Temptress*?"

"Why don't you tell me which one you're going to pick?"

Michael studied the program for several minutes.

"I'm going to pick *Popcorn*," said Michael.

"Because you love popcorn?"

"No, because he usually does well on the turf and he won his last seven-furlong race."

Julia laughed. "I'll do two on *Popcorn* as well, then."

"Look, there's Mr. Clark," said Michael. Jim and several other policemen were at a booth giving away sheriff stars to children. "He lives across the street from me."

"He does? I didn't know that. Are you close?"

"No." Michael squinted in the sun. "I don't like him much."

"Why not?"

"He yells. And Tina's weird."

"His daughter? Is that the one who meets you by the fence during recess?" Michael nodded. "Weird how?" she asked.

Michael thought. "Sometimes she's really nice and sometimes she's not at all. Same as him."

Julia looked over to Jim. He held court among the men and children, making a plastic sheriff star disappear and then reappear to giggles and squeals. He smiled broadly, but there was no warmth. He looked like a grown-up doll, shellac over plastic.

He caught Julia staring and stopped his show to walk over, keeping his eyes on her the whole way.

"Hello, Julia," he said, extending a hand. "Good to see you." Then he noticed Michael and smiled so widely his cheeks grew apples. "Mike, my boy! How's it going?" The two had not spoken since he kicked Michael out of his yard.

"Fine."

"Did you know my horse is over there? Go pet it, tell them I said it was okay." He motioned for Michael to leave, and because Julia did not protest, Michael did.

They watched Michael reach the horses, and then Jim said, "Good day for the races."

"Yes," Julia said, and she pushed her hair behind her ear. "I should probably go—"

"Let's have a drink sometime. You can tell me about teaching, and I'll tell you about all the crazy things I see that never make the papers." His black eyes sparkled, and Julia looked away, back to Michael.

"I don't think that would be a good idea."

"Why not?"

"You're married."

He waved her off. "Cassie wouldn't mind. Just a friendly drink. Nothing to get all worked up about."

"Thank you, but no." She glanced up as far as his mouth and nose. "I have to go." She walked to Michael, and as she led him back to their seats, she looked back. Jim was watching her with a satisfied smile that made Julia wonder if she'd actually said yes.

She looked back, Jim thought. He returned to his colleagues, who chuckled and grunted when he told them that the young new teacher in town had asked him over for drinks, even though he was married.

"Balls on that woman," they said. "Will you do it?"

"It would be rude not to," he said, and he laughed.

Julia was homesick for Rose when she returned home that afternoon. She was full of things, none of which came out when she sat down to write Rose another letter.

I had the most fabulous time with Michael at the races today. The horses were beautiful, and I felt perfectly a part of a Maurice Taquoy painting, but all of that was superficial. Really, I felt sorry for the poor things. It was so hot, and I wonder if the whips hurt? They must, else why would they use them?

Michael won $30! I walked away with $10 (mostly due to Michael's advice). He offered to give me some of his winnings, which I declined. So he bought me an ice cream cone. He is such a dear.

I have decided I'll do whatever it takes to make Michael happy and feel welcome here. He's out of place, he's hurting, and it seems he has no one to turn to.

We ran into Jim Clark, the officer I told you about. It was the only black spot on an otherwise wonderful day.
Love,
Julia

Thirteen

The following day, Michael kneeled in his shed that looked like a barn, tightening the screws on his bicycle. It wasn't broken or even wobbly, but he enjoyed working with his hands, something he realized only after he'd moved off the farm and the necessity of it was gone. He looked up to see Tina walking across the backyard.

"Hey," she said, standing in the open doorway, and Michael smiled at her.

"Why did you go to the racetrack with Miss Parnell yesterday?" she asked. Her eyebrows were furrowed in a way that suggested to Michael her question was not innocent.

He shrugged. "For fun."

"Fun with your teacher?"

"Yeah."

"What do you talk about?"

"Just things."

"Like what?"

He was getting annoyed and stopped fidgeting with his bike. "I don't know."

Tina leaned toward him with her head, much like a turtle. "You're so gay," she said.

"Leave me alone."

Tina laughed. "Seriously. Who hangs out with their teacher?"

Michael didn't respond, wrenched a screw that didn't need

wrenching, wished she would leave. He hated it when she was in these moods.

"Don't have a cow, I'm just trying to help you." She snapped a daisy growing at her feet off its stem and placed it in her hair. "I heard your teacher has sex with women."

Michael blushed and looked up at Tina despite himself.

"Well, does she?" asked Tina.

"How do I know?"

"I thought you were her best friend."

"No." The wrench clinked against the metal.

"Well, my mom heard from some chick at the salon who knows someone who said she heard that Miss Parnell's a lesbian and used to live with a woman. She said someone should find out for sure, since she's teaching kids." Tina eyed Michael, who was trying hard to look disinterested.

"Anyway, it's gross, don't you think?"

"Sure." Michael dropped his wrench. "I have to go wash up before supper."

"'Supper.'" Tina laughed. "You're so funny."

Later, Michael lay on his stomach on the family room floor, sketching in the pad he got for his birthday last year. It was half filled with long-ago images from their farm—the cow, the fields, the oak tree. Michael was under the impression that he cheated, since he reproduced only what he saw. He could never draw from memory, so he had none of the wolves he'd seen with his father; only wolves from books and, like his current drawing, from the cover of his *National Geographic*.

His mother walked in, carrying a basket full of laundry up to her chin. She dumped the laundry on the couch and sat down to fold. This was a relaxing chore for her, smoothing wrinkles and folding the clothes into squares.

"How is Miss Parnell?" she asked.

"Good."

"I'm so glad it's working out. It makes me feel better while I'm at work."

"She lets me help her during recess, too," said Michael. "And after school."

Anne set down the shirt she'd been folding.

"I know you are probably going through a hard time right now," she said. "You're a good boy, Michael. That doesn't always mean things will be easy."

"Whatever," he snapped, and his mother looked wounded.

"What do you mean, whatever?" she asked.

But Michael didn't know what he meant. He just knew that every time his mother told him things would get easier, or that things weren't supposed to be easy, or that he should do this or that, he felt like screaming.

That week, Julia received her first letter from Rose since she left Iowa two months before.

> *Dear Julia,*
> *How can you do it? Michael, Jim Clark, lesson plans, shop-ping trips, weather? Don't you know I don't care about any of that?*
> *You can't just step into a new life; you can't just be another person.*
> *Rose*

> *Dear Rose,*
> *My feelings have not changed. You said sometimes the hardest thing is the right thing, but what if both choices are the hardest thing?*

You may think I am weak or a coward. Maybe I am. But I'm doing what I know how to do. I'm living and teaching and breathing in and out and sometimes I think I'll die but I won't.
Love,
Julia

Fourteen

Julia's only friend in town was a nine-year-old boy. If she wanted to include anyone she talked to, she supposed she could count Andy or the other teachers she spoke to in the teachers' lounge. Or the mailman she passed on the street.

She could join her colleagues for a drink after work any of the Fridays they regularly went to Murphy's, but she couldn't think of anything worse. Questions about her past, her relationships, her life. The answers she'd have to give, the ones they would expect. She was not yet strong enough to begin stacking the bricks around her again.

Michael's youth provided a gulf between them that she would not have with a more mature friendship. Or perhaps she was fooling herself into thinking one could not really be close with a nine-year-old.

On the first cold afternoon of autumn, a Saturday, Julia invited Michael to meet her at the drug store for hot chocolate. She waited for him at the end of the counter, as most of the stools were taken up by the usual cadre of men. The door opened, letting in a rush of cool air, and Jim Clark walked in. He nodded at Julia and watched her from where he stood at the other end of the counter. He listened to the men around him, but his eyes did not move from her. She was sure he was about to walk over when Michael arrived. Julia met him near the entrance and shuffled him toward the corner door that led to her apartment. "Let's have some snacks upstairs," she said. "They're out of hot chocolate."

In her kitchen, Julia found milk and chocolate sauce, which

she warmed in a pan on the stove. She carried a tray of cheese and crackers into the living room, where Michael was watching an episode of *Three's Company*.

"I'm not sure your mother would like you watching this," Julia said, walking to the television to turn it off. "Let's just visit."

"Who's that?" asked Michael, pointing to a framed picture on the table next to the couch. He stuffed his mouth with a cracker.

"That's Rose," said Julia, sitting down next to him. "She's my friend."

"Where does she live?"

"A few hours away, in Iowa where I used to live."

"Did you live with her?"

Julia was a bit surprised by the question. "Yes, I did. We'd been friends since we were little girls in Kansas."

"Oh," said Michael. "So she wasn't your girlfriend?"

Julia took a sharp breath. Where was this coming from? Was he just making random connections, as children do? Or had he heard something?

"No," she said. "Would it be so bad if she was?" She tried to make a joke of it, but it was clumsy and harsh.

"I don't know," said Michael. His large brown eyes watched her.

Julia felt shame then, prickling down from her ears and along her neck, her insecurities laid bare. He simply wanted to know. Nothing more.

"I've known Rose my whole life," she began. "She's not my girlfriend, but I've probably loved her since I was five years old. It's hard to understand."

Michael shook his head. "No, I understand. My mother says she still loves my father, even though they're not together."

Julia smiled. "That's right."

"Why didn't she come with you?"

Julia crossed her legs and fidgeted with the hem of her skirt, running her nail along its edge, letting the blue checked pattern distract her for a moment. "It was hard."

"Why?"

She knew she shouldn't continue speaking but she wanted to, suddenly. She wanted to share something with this boy, her friend. She wanted to tell him the truth.

Her words were chosen and careful. "Some people think it's not right because it's not what usually happens. Not everybody could accept us living together. Not everybody would be able to here, either." She wanted to make that clear without asking him to lie, to keep her secret. "Do you understand?"

Michael nodded. He thought he did.

Fifteen

Tina had watched Michael and Miss Parnell walk through the door that led up to the teacher's apartment. She'd just arrived at the drugstore to fetch her dad, who had forgotten to mow the lawn. But Jim wasn't ready to leave, and Tina did not want to have to explain that to her mom. So she sat on a bench outside the drugstore and waited. Watching the people walk past, in and out of shops, Tina wondered at all the different errands. It was like the time she and her mom ran into Mrs. Wilderhausen at the grocery store. As the two women talked, Tina looked at Mrs. Wilderhausen's cart. It was filled with items Tina did not recognize—strange fruit and spaetzle and cans of sauerkraut. No Hostess cupcakes or cheese sandwich crackers. Mrs. Wilderhausen lived right across the street and had a whole different life, she realized.

Tina was biting the last of her fingernails down to the quick when Michael walked past on his way out the door an hour later. She caught up with him.

"Hey," she said, and they walked in silence for a few moments. "I'm sorry about what I said the other day. I don't think you're gay."

Michael remained quiet.

"Do you want to come over?" she asked.

"I can't."

"Can I come to your house?"

"I have homework. Maybe tomorrow."

"Hey, some kid caught a frog in the field yesterday during recess. He and another boy played catch with it."

Michael looked up, his face red. "That's mean."

"I know," said Tina. "I thought so, too."

At 7:00 PM that evening, after finding nothing on television while she waited for her parents, Tina left her house and rang the Nygaard's doorbell. She stood on the front stoop with one hand holding her elbow behind her back when Mrs. Nygaard came to the door.

"Hello, Tina. How are you?" she said.

"I was wondering if I could come over for dinner tonight."

Anne glanced across the street at Tina's house. "I'll have to check with your parents."

"They're not home."

Anne opened the screen door to let Tina in. "Of course you're welcome. We already finished, but I can heat up some leftovers. And we've got strawberry shortcake for dessert."

She called Michael back to the table while she served Tina real mashed potatoes, roasted carrots, and slices of chicken. The leftovers were gleaming and steamy, heaps of rich food. Tina was conscious of the silverware, the nice plates, even for dessert; she noticed that Michael placed a napkin on his lap. It was hard for Tina to imagine that people ate this way on any regular day of the week.

As Anne whipped the cream at the counter for the strawberry shortcake, Tina leaned over and whispered to Michael, "Sorry. I was starving."

"It's okay."

Tina was comforted in the quiet except the whirring of the blender in Anne's hand. Gentle movements, gentle air, the whole kitchen reminded Tina of the soft little peaks of whipped cream, and she sank into her chair. As they ate their shortcake, Tina lived in the simple statements, simply spoken.

"I spoke with your uncle today," said Anne. "He's going to find a lake nearby."

"I wonder if they have northerns here."

"I'm sure they do."

"Dad would know."

"Your uncle will know."

Michael didn't mind waiting for Uncle Kevin to take him fishing; in the long dull days, it was a bright spot in the distance. As long as it was there, he had something to look forward to, just like his visit to Minnesota. Thoughts of it carried his mind away from here.

When dessert was over, Tina did not want to leave, but it was time for Michael to wash up for bed.

"Are your parents home, yet?" asked Anne, peering out the front window.

"Dunno," said Tina. "But it's okay."

After she walked out the front door, Tina went to the back of the house and looked in the window. The kitchen chair where she had just been sitting was pushed out from the table. Whipped cream and crumbs spotted the placemats. Happy little crumbs. Michael and his mother remained, speaking softly, Tina knew, even though she could not hear. Tina was searching for a reason to go back inside and sit with them when Anne stood and cupped Michael's cheek with a hand, then brought her plate to the sink. Michael cleared the rest of the table as his mother washed dishes. Tina walked away only when they left the room.

The next night, Tina came back. Anne didn't bother asking about her parents. She opened the screen door and welcomed Tina inside to pot roast and silverware and napkins. *Tina*, Anne thought, *must be a lonely child.* Something she shared with the girl, she noted. Sometimes Anne looked out across the neighborhood from her front step and imagined what it looked like many years before, in the game she, John, and Michael used to play. She wanted to know, to feel some connection to the earth that her home was now grounded on. This earth had sustained life for millions of years, and now she was living on it, was being sustained. There must be some connection to be made. But she did not feel it. Not with the land nor the numerous houses upon it.

Even Anne could see, from her spot across the street, that Tina struggled for attention. Whenever the family pulled into their driveway and exited the car, Anne waved. Cassie waved back if Jim wasn't there. They'd never actually communicated beyond waves. If Jim was there, Cassie's attention was often on him, following him into the house, Tina walking in last. That always bothered Anne—neither parent ever held the door for Tina to go through. If the two carried on that way inside the home as well, Tina must be lost.

"I understand your mother works at a salon nearby. Which one?" asked Anne, as she placed a slice of meat on Tina's plate.

"Veronica's. It's a shit job." Tina looked at Anne and Michael. "Sorry."

Anne waved her away. "It's alright. Michael has needed soap in his mouth before, too. I remember when he was six and just started first grade."

"Mom," said Michael.

"He came home one day and told me his teacher assigned 'too much damn homework.'" She turned to Michael. "You thought you were all grown up." She laughed at the memory, but Tina blushed. Only yesterday she had said the same thing.

"And your father?" asked Anne. "How does he like the police force?"

Tina shrugged. "He doesn't work a lot lately. He hurt his back."

"Oh, I'm sorry to hear that."

"He can still walk and stuff. It's just sore."

"That must be nice to have your father home more."

Tina didn't respond, and Anne was embarrassed.

Michael was quiet. The voices of his mother and Tina were

behind him, to the side of him, muffled, and he watched his father at the other end of the table listening to the conversation with a smile on his face. He turned to Michael and said, "This one's got horns holding up her halo, doesn't she?" and laughed. Then Tina clinked her glass against her plate as she set it down and Michael was brought back, his father gone.

After Tina left, when his mother commented that it was nice to have a friend just across the street, Michael said, "She can be mean sometimes."

This didn't surprise Anne. "That girl's enduring hardship," she said, scrubbing dishes at the sink. "It's spread all over her."

Michael wondered then what hardship included. He felt he was enduring something like it, yet he didn't call people names or yell at them or make them feel foolish, like Tina did.

As Michael left the drug store late one afternoon, Tina appeared next to him from seemingly nowhere, as she often did.

"You weren't outside the school again," she said as they fell in step together. "I waited."

"I went to Miss Parnell's. She just got the coolest game." He adjusted his backpack straps on his shoulders. A mass of books caused the backpack to sag and thump against his backside as he walked.

"What game?" asked Tina.

"Frogger. It's a video game you play on your TV."

"I know. What, are you from outer space?"

Michael was unfazed. "I'd never heard of it."

"I play all the time."

"You do? Where?"

"In our basement. We've had it forever."

Michael doubted this was true but didn't say that. "You should come with next time. Miss Parnell said I could bring a friend."

Tina rolled her eyes. "No, thanks. I'm not hanging out with your homo teacher."

"She's not a homo."

"My mom said she is." Tina stooped quickly to pick a tall dandelion growing in a crack of the cement.

"She's not," said Michael. "It's not like that."

Tina turned sideways toward Michael as they walked. "What do you mean? What's not like that? Oh my God, you asked her?"

"No. She told me."

Tina gasped. "What did she say?"

Michael shrugged. "She has a friend named Rose."

"Friend? Or girlfriend?" asked Tina.

"Friend. She said she loves someone named Rose and they lived together."

Tina stopped walking for a moment and then ran to catch up. "So it's true! I can't believe your teacher is a homo. My mom's never right about anything."

Michael walked faster, looking straight toward home. He didn't know what was happening. "No. It's not true. She's not a homo."

"What do you mean? She loves a girl. That's a homo."

"Stop it! It's not how you said. You're just being mean!"

"Whatever." But Tina knew. She was appalled and thrilled. She'd never actually known a homosexual. She hadn't imagined they looked anything like Miss Parnell, but then her mom was always telling her to be careful, that people weren't always what they appeared to be.

"It's okay," said Tina. "I won't tell."

And she meant it. As far as she knew, she and Michael were the only ones who knew whether Miss Parnell was gay—not her mother, not the town, not the school. She would show Michael that she could keep this secret they shared. She and Michael.

The next night, Tina came for dinner. But when Mrs. Nygaard answered the door, she told Tina that they were already finished and there was nothing left for her to have. Tina stood on the front step a moment, looking at the closed door. Then she walked around to the back of the house. She watched Michael and his mother clean up together, then followed outside as they walked to the family room to watch television. They sat side by side. She remembered Michael saying once that he and his mother were sad, that things were different. That made her mad now as she stood in the grass at the window, just outside the light.

Sixteen

The sun was well over the horizon, but it did little to warm the father and son sitting in the woods. They had been watching for over an hour, and the chill began to creep into Michael's fingers and toes. A white-gray sky sprinkled tiny bits of dry snow that bounced when they landed, reminding Michael of the inside of the stuffed bunny he used to carry around, the one he and Pike "dissected" in second grade.

He'd always liked hearing his father talk, the deep voice vibrating, a sound Michael wanted to touch. He often fell asleep at night to his voice out in the kitchen. Here in the woods, sitting small and surrounded by trees, Michael received what his father offered—the clearing, the stories, his voice. And it felt like church to him.

Tentatively, he asked for more.

"What was Grandpa like?" he said.

"Gosh," said his father, rubbing the cold out of his thighs. "Hard to say. He was quiet. But when he did talk, to tell you the truth, he was kind of a bully."

"He was?" This surprised Michael, to know someone so close to his father could be so different.

John nodded. "He never hit me. Sometimes I wished he would have. The other stuff was hard to take."

"What other stuff?"

"Oh, I don't want to get into that. He's your grandpa."

"I never knew him anyway."

His father drew his knees toward his chest—he was such a big man they came nowhere near—and continued watching the den site. "One summer, when I was about your age, I befriended a little mouse, so to speak. He was easy to spot from the others, had a brown head and a gray body. Funny looking mouse. I started leaving crumbs for it. He'd come and eat while I was brushing the horses or milking. He never let me touch him, but he always came to eat when I was there. So I got it in my head that he came to see me. And I started creating reasons to go to the barn.

"My father didn't like animals. If he could have had a farm without them, he would have. He thought they smelled, called them stupid creatures. One day, I was pretending to brush the horses while watching the mouse eat in the corner near the door. My father was outside shoveling the pens. I'd taken to talking to the mouse, having just read *Charlotte's Web*. I was hoping maybe I'd hear something back," he said, and smiled at the thought. "My voice must have drawn him in because he appeared suddenly at the door with his shovel. He looked at the mouse, then back at me. 'Don't be such a sissy,' he said and scooped up the mouse and tossed it behind him into the middle of a group of farmyard cats. That was that."

Michael's chest hurt. "What did Grandma say?"

"She didn't know."

"Was he mean to her, too?"

"Heck no. She wouldn't allow it."

In truth, John's earliest memory was looking in a window, watching his father beat his mother on the floor. His mother blamed the alcohol, said it wasn't really him. He didn't drink often, so the episodes were rare enough to make her think it true. She sent little John and his younger brothers to the woods when he came home drunk, so they were spared. It was there in the woods one night that John heard his first wolf howl. He was not scared and knew even then that was remarkable. The wolf told John, huddled under a pine with his arms wrapped around his brothers, that he was safe.

"No wonder he wasn't mean to her," said Michael. "She shot wolves."

"Sure did."

"I bet there were a lot more back then."

His father nodded. "We've done a pretty good job of wiping them out. Not deer, though." He nodded at the den site. "I think that's why these wolves haven't had to move around. Plenty to eat. Far as I know, they've used this site several springs in a row."

All of a sudden, in a flutter, five wolves came from behind the hill and walked horizontally along it to the den, disappearing one by one inside an opening Michael hadn't known was there. And then they were gone.

"It's almost like seeing the history of the Earth, in a wolf," said his father.

"Yes," he replied, though it had happened so fast he felt let down. But he wouldn't have told his father that. "Which ones were they?"

"The large gray one in front was the alpha male. The blacker alpha female was right behind, followed by the two adolescents from last year's brood, both females. The last one, the one that was almost white, was one of alpha's brothers." But his father was distracted. He kept his eyes on the hill searching, waiting for something.

"The omega wasn't with them," he said, finally. "He's gone."

Michael stood on the sidewalk in front of the Clark house, waiting for his mother. He felt sorry he'd asked her to turn Tina away last night, and so he persuaded her to come with him to invite Tina over tonight. He told his mother he just felt awkward inviting a girl to dinner, though really he didn't want to go to the Clarks' by himself. He wished his mother would hurry up.

Through the screen door several yards away, he heard Cassie yell. "Right in front of me, Jim? In front of Tina?"

Then Jim: "Oh my God, this is the worst thing in the world. You have the worst husband in the world."

"You disrespected me."

"Please. You don't need me for that."

Michael inched up the driveway, unable to help himself. He could see half of the kitchen table through the screen.

Jim sat down and opened a beer.

"Have another," said Cassie, out of view. "It's what you do best lately."

"Give me a break. You don't know what I deal with all day."

"Tell me, Jim. What do you deal with? Too many parking tickets?"

"Go to hell."

Cassie chuckled. "All jittery like a damn teenager. You're making a fool of yourself."

He slammed an open hand on the table and Michael started. "Jesus, do you ever shut up?"

It was quiet for a moment. Michael thought the argument was over and he stood, wondering whether he should just walk back home. *Tina must not even be inside*, he thought. Then he saw Jim pull Cassie down onto his lap. Cassie winced as he grabbed a fistful of short hair above the nape of her neck and pulled back. He kissed her throat, upward along her jawline, and then engulfed her mouth with his. Michael stood wide-eyed. This must be what Tina had talked about.

Cassie pulled away. "I'm not in the mood."

But Jim pushed her mouth back to his and Cassie sat still, hands in lap. Jim took one of her hands and placed it on his head, moving it in a circle until Cassie performed the act on her own, her red fingernails tousling his hair while they kissed. Then Jim's free hand reached under her T-shirt to her chest, and Michael fled, anxious to get back to his own home.

When Tina heard her parents go to their room and shut the door, she went outside. She knew what they'd be doing and for how long.

Instead of ringing the Nygaard's doorbell, she just walked around to the back of the house and looked through the kitchen window. She didn't want to be turned away again. As she watched, mother and son ate together, cleaned up together, and played cards together. She could not make out the conversation but watched as they spoke continuously, alternately laying down cards. She wondered if Mrs. Nygaard ever yelled, but knew she probably did not. She wondered what Mr. Nygaard had been like, and could easily imagine a third quiet person in this scene, a larger version of Michael. Big and quiet, small and quiet.

It was now familiar, this feeling that flooded Tina when she watched them. She was in love with the feeling, one she could not name even if she thought about it, for she had never felt it before. She would stand outside the window every night if it meant she could have this feeling. She would bring a blanket and snacks, and remember mittens so her hands weren't cold. She would sit when she was tired of standing and be cozy, safe among the bushes.

"What are you doing?" Michael asked. He stood a few feet from her. She hadn't noticed when he left the kitchen. Mrs. Nygaard peered out through the window.

"Nothing," said Tina, and paused for a moment, what felt like a long moment, and she thought maybe he would shrug and ask her to come inside. But he just stood there, staring, and so she ran home, her eyes beginning to drip with tears, her head pounding.

When Tina burst in, Cassie sat at the kitchen table drinking a beer. Mascara pooled beneath her eyes, and she did not seem to notice her daughter had been crying as well.

"Your father left," she said.

"What do you mean?" Tina stood near the door wiping her cheeks.

"I mean he's gone. We were fine, we fought, he threw on his

clothes, and he left. I don't know where, probably to the damn drug store." She patted a kitchen chair. "Come sit with me."

Tina climbed into the chair next to her mother.

"Here," she said, pushing her beer over to Tina. "I'll let you have a sip. It'll make you feel better, too, whatever's wrong."

Tina drank and slid the beer back to her mother.

Cassie watched her daughter. "Do you want to get married, Tina?" she asked.

After an imperceptible shrug, Tina said, "Don't know."

"I want you to want to get married. It's so much easier to get through life with someone. Your dad and I used to have a good marriage. I wish you could've seen."

"I know."

"I want you to be happy. I want to be able to show you how."

They sat in silence for a few minutes until Cassie continued. "When I was younger, I had to turn men away." She smiled and looked at Tina. "You probably don't believe that about your mom, do you? The girls and I, we didn't even have to try. Easy as pie." She stared into her beer. "You act like you don't care about anything but hanging out with the girls, like you don't care who else is in the bar. You're just there to have fun with your friends. But you throw it in their faces. Maybe wear a low-cut shirt, something that shows just enough of your chest to get them thinking. Or a short skirt." She held up a hand. "Not slutty, never slutty. But short enough they can imagine themselves there. You don't let them get that far, of course. Not at first. But you want them to be able to imagine it. Once they imagine it, they're yours." She looked at her daughter as she took a sip. "Make them want you, Tina."

Tina found Michael sitting on a stool inside the shed in his back yard, whittling wood away from his mother's view.

"Can I come in?" she asked.

"Suit yourself."

It was the end of October, and after some chilly days, Indian summer had come. The air was sticky and hot inside the shed. A little light came in from the cracked door, and dust floated in its rays. Tina watched as Michael sliced one long curl of wood after another, mesmerized by the slow, repeated motions.

"Aren't you scared you'll cut yourself?"

"If you get it right, it's like cool butter." He'd heard his father say that once.

Outside, a lone cicada screamed its existence. Tina loved their loud songs, pulsing and frantic yet somehow calming. She was sorry that soon their music would be gone for the winter.

"Don't be mad at me," she said, and she sat down on a half-empty gas can. Her fingers twisted the jelly bracelets on her arm.

"I'm not mad at you," said Michael. "I just don't know why you were standing outside the window."

She shrugged. "I was just watching."

"Watching what?"

"You and your mom. Playing cards."

"Why?"

"I don't know." She knew what she was here to do, though she did not yet know how she was going to do it, and she didn't want to be talking about the window. She wanted to forget the window. "What are you making?" she asked.

"Nothing. Just slicing a stick."

"Like a spear."

"Yeah. My dad used to whittle. We had sticks like this lying all over the farm."

"What for?"

"Dunno. He just liked to do it. My mom hated it. She said the sticks were dangerous. I don't know how they could be, though, unless you picked one up and poked yourself in the eye." They laughed.

"Was your dad like you?"

"Me?" He thought. He'd never had to describe his dad before. He didn't know how to say what he was like, knew only what he did. "He used to let me drive sometimes. And I helped him plant soybeans. He took me with him to watch his wolves. He loved wolves. And he was really smart, always talking about things like a book does."

"Was he quiet, like you?"

"Yeah. Except . . ." A picture was forming in his head.

"Except what?"

"At my baseball games, I could always hear his voice cheering over all the others. He was loud then."

Tina was comfortable now. It was the right moment.

"Boy, it's hot," she said. Michael nodded in agreement.

She pulled her shirt over her head, exposing her naked torso. "This is cooler."

Michael looked up and his face flushed with blood. "What are you doing?"

"It's too hot in here. I don't have anything, anyway, so it doesn't matter. It only matters once you need a bra." She looked at him closer and laughed. "Your face is red." Michael looked away.

Tina brushed her hands over her chest. "It's no big deal. I only have little ones. Here, do you want to feel?" She reached out for his hand.

"No!" he said, and moved away. He did not know what to say, so he looked back down and tried to continue whittling. But he was nervous now, and his hands were sweating. The knife slipped and cut into his finger. Blood oozed out, and he gasped.

"Here, I'll fix it," said Tina. She wrapped her shirt around his hand and squeezed to stop the blood.

"Take off your shirt," she said.

"No!"

"So I can wear it outside, silly. You got mine all bloody."

Slowly, he pulled his shirt over his head and handed it to her. As she grabbed it, she leaned over to kiss him on the mouth. He jumped back.

"Why don't you want to kiss me?" asked Tina.

"I don't know."

"It's okay. I'll show you how."

"I don't want to."

"It's fun."

He shook his head.

This was not supposed to happen. Tina stood half-naked while Michael looked repelled by her. "You're such a baby," she said, and she pulled Michael's shirt over her head, though it was inside out. "Just a little baby." She rushed out, thinking, *How dare he?*

She ran toward town, loving the pound of every footstep against the pavement. Screw Michael, screw Michael, screw Michael. She pumped her fists, pushing the air upward as she passed the cleaners and Baskin-Robbins, and then she was stopped by the sound of her father's voice through the open door of the drugstore. He stood in a circle with other men, his back to her. She listened, breathing heavily as she leaned against the glass storefront.

"Oh, for the days when I could have had some of that," said Mr. Wilderhausen.

"I'm going to *have* some of that," said Jim.

"You've been saying that for weeks now."

"I can't just jump her the first time we have drinks together."

Steve Lubbock spoke up. "You've been out with her?"

"Yep." Jim took a swig from his cup.

"What does your wife think about that?" asked Steve.

"Who cares," said Jim. "It won't be long before I have that sweet young lady on her knees." He pointed to his pants, and the men laughed.

Tina walked into the store, slow and deliberate. She knew who they were talking about. She didn't want her dad to make a fool of himself, like her mom said he would. She walked toward him, through naughty words slung about in the air, words she knew but didn't want to know, words that often drifted through the wall from her parents' room, until the laughter stopped into silence and she stood before her dad.

"Don't like her," she said.

He turned to see Tina and then glanced at the others, embarrassed. "What?"

"Don't like Miss Parnell."

"Why?"

"Because she's a lezbo. She has a girlfriend."

The other men snorted, chuckling into their cups. Jim ignored them, though his ears burned. "Where'd you get a thing like that?"

"Mom."

"Huh!" Jim relaxed. "Your mother will say anything. Always been jealous." He took another drink and set his cup on the counter. "See you tomorrow, boys." Placing his hands on her shoulders, he led Tina out the door.

When they were outside walking down the block in the bright sun, he said, "Don't come in there like that again, talking about things you don't know."

"The ladies at the salon told her."

"Get a group of girls together in a room and what you have is a whole pile of bullshit."

"And Michael," said Tina. "Michael told me, too."

The next day, Tina sat on her bed playing solitaire. The cards were skewed on her ruffled comforter, but she was barely paying attention. Her dad knocked about in the kitchen; her mom had gone to the salon a few hours ago. That reminded Tina to look under her pillow, and she found a shiny purple rock. Smiling, she turned it over in her hand several times before placing it in a bowl on her bedside table.

Her father had been home all day again, even though he was supposed to work Sundays. The banging in the kitchen annoyed her, so she leaned over to her boom box and put in The Police.

"Christina!" her father called from the kitchen, his voice deep and loud, cutting through her music like a cello off key.

Tina slid off the bed, a few cards dropping to the floor. She walked down the hall to the kitchen, where her father stood at the counter rifling through bills and piles of paper.

"Get your stuff," he said.

"What stuff?"

"Your purse, whatever."

"Daddy, I don't have a purse," Tina laughed.

"We need to run to the drugstore."

Tina whined. "I don't want to go sit at the drugstore."

"I'm not staying. I just need Coke." He jiggled a bowl of change, spilling coins onto the counter.

Tina glanced at the empty beer cans on the table, the full bottle of rum.

Her dad opened a drawer and pushed aside its contents. "Aha!" He held the car keys in the air. "Let's go!"

After several tries, he parallel parked the car in front of the drug store, though the back right wheel was up on the curb. When Tina pointed it out from the sidewalk, he waved her away. He opened the door to the store and stood face-to-face with Miss Parnell, who was on her way out.

"Well, speak of the devil," he said. "It's Miss Parnell. Lovely Miss Parnell."

"Hello," Miss Parnell answered with a half smile, and she continued on, but he grabbed her arm.

"Why so short?" he said. "Can't you stop and have a friendly chat?" He leaned in close and lowered his voice. "What about that drink you promised me?"

"I never promised you a drink."

"There's a rumor you're a faggot. Ladies at the salon are talking about it. Tina's talking about it. But I say a pretty lady like you couldn't be."

"Dad," said Tina, grabbing his other hand, but he ignored her.

The hair by Miss Parnell's ear fluttered against the weight of his breath. "I know girls like to fool around with each other once in a while, and that's okay. I think it's sexy. A dyke, on the other hand, is disgusting."

"Dad," Tina said again, pulling on his arm. She didn't want to blink or the tears would show.

He moved in closer, his nose touching Miss Parnell's ear. "It's not true, is it?"

"This is inappropriate," said Miss Parnell, her arm pulling against his hold.

"Answer me," he said. "Is it true?"

"Let go of me *now*."

Jim stared at Miss Parnell a few seconds before letting go. "I guess it is," he said. He grabbed Tina's hand and shoved past the teacher, pushing Tina through the door toward rows of soda and candy and several onlookers.

Seventeen

Indian summer was over. The sun shone through the last of the leaves, which had long lost the deep green opaque of summer. The maples were almost translucent now, allowing the sun's rays to poke through bit by bit until in as little as a week the chartreuse luster would burn gold and red and join the others on the ground. Julia wore a light jacket as she stood outside the drugstore after school waiting for Michael to arrive for ice cream.

She watched him as he approached from down the block. She'd thought all week about her confrontation with Jim Clark. She knew Michael must have said something to Tina, knew it could only be him. But she felt a floating pause, as though maybe, again, it would all blow over, around and above her.

When Michael stood before her with pinked cheeks and his hands in his coat pockets, he said, "Can we just go inside and get hot chocolate?"

Julia paused for a moment before nodding. "Good idea."

She opened the drug store door, and they walked inside together. Everyone turned, as they usually did when anyone came in. Upon seeing Julia with Michael, the men went back to what they were doing, all except Jim Clark.

Julia walked toward the other end of the counter. Michael followed and jumped into the last open stool.

"Hi, Andy," said Julia.

"Hey, Julia, what can I do for you?"

She could feel Jim Clark's eyes on her, and her lips were numb as she spoke. "Two hot chocolates, please."

"Sure thing. Whipped cream?"

"Of course." Julia fiddled with her purse, looking for money.

Andy grabbed two large ceramic cups from under the counter. "Which one of you gentlemen is gonna get up so the lady can have a seat?" he called down the row.

"Oh, really, it's okay," said Julia. "I've been sitting all day." Andy offered her an apologetic smile when no one moved.

"You can sit here," said Michael.

"Thank you, Michael, that is very sweet," said Julia. "But I'd rather stand." She tried not to look at the other end of the counter.

"Know what I read the other day?" Jim asked of Steve Lubbock next to him, but loud enough so everyone at the counter could hear. "I read that little kids are getting AIDS from bad transfusions—the bad blood of homo donors. Now they're spreading it to innocents."

"You're kidding?" said Steve.

"At first I didn't care." Jim shrugged. "Just God's way of putting things back in a natural order—bring on a disease for the gays. It made sense. But now kids are getting it."

"That's criminal. Someone needs to do something about that."

"Michael, let's take our hot chocolates upstairs," said Julia. "It'll be much warmer up there, and we can play cards."

Michael stood and they walked together toward the rear door.

Jim went after them, grinning. He reached the two just as Julia opened the door and Michael walked through. Holding the door open, he motioned for Julia to follow Michael and then placed his other hand on the opposite side of the doorframe. His smile disappeared.

"Dyke," he said.

Julia could sense Michael's eyes widen. She felt the weight of the room begin to spiral into her.

"Watch your mouth," she said. "Did you come over here just to say that?"

Jim was smug. "It was more of a question. Things were a little hazy the other day, but I'm pretty sure you still haven't denied it."

"I'll deny it now, Mr. Clark. I am not gay."

But his grin reappeared as he crossed his arms and leaned against the doorframe, holding the door open with his foot. "I have it on pretty good authority that you are," he said.

"From whom?" But she knew the answer. And though she wanted to succumb to the weight pushing her down, let it melt her into the floor, she was somehow able to suspend belief, to hope, to force him to say he'd made it all up.

Jim nodded at Michael. "From him."

Before she could help it, Julia's shoulders slumped in exhale and her eyes flickered toward Michael in disappointment. She knew from his face that he thought he did something terribly wrong; it showed confusion and sadness and shame all mixed together. And she had created that for him.

"I'm sorry," said Michael, his eyebrows furrowed. "Tina said, but I . . ." He swallowed and stuffed his hands back into his pockets. "I didn't think it was wrong."

And for some reason, at that moment, Julia thought of high school and the girl who wanted to ban the book. She remembered she'd told her mother the story later, told her how appalled she was and how un-American it seemed, but really she'd wanted her mother to know she had stood up in front of all those people and spoken her opinion.

But her mother hadn't said, "My word!" She'd looked at Julia with patronizing confusion, the way she looked at waitresses when they forgot to put the dressing on the side, and said, "It doesn't matter that you think you're right, Julia. *They* think you're wrong."

And that was that. It became Julia's truth without Julia ever knowing she'd decided that was the way it would be.

But standing in front of Michael and Jim Clark, for the first time she recognized the power and the malfeasance of those words—*it doesn't matter that you think you're right*. Not in a million years would she have said them to Michael. Julia watched Michael stand-ing before her ashamed and realized in one sweeping instant who she was. And who she wasn't. To thine own self be true. Wherever you go, go with all your heart. She was the person she would have told Michael not to be. It was somehow startling to discover this.

And then it was clear, so that she was unable to see how she could have ever considered it differently, how she could have ever let the words rule over her.

Dear Rose,
It's out. You were right. It has followed me around like a
hungry dog, and there is no kicking it away.
Love,
Julia

How does one begin to live differently?

Focus on every thought? Consider every decision? And then *move*, not simply think?

Julia had no idea. She had dirty dishes in the sink and a list of groceries to buy. She had next week's lesson plans to write and yes-terday's papers to grade.

She grabbed a red pen, turned over her grade sheet to the blank side, and made a list. It was a teacherly thing to do. If she was going to start believing, as Michael did, that she was right, she needed to figure out what else she might have gotten wrong. "Leaving Rose" was at the top. "Not telling" was next—she listed her parents, her friends, her coworkers. And then, with sudden recognition, she added, "Me." She had the thought to write "I am gay" on the sheet, to just get it out, and started with "I" but felt stopped up, so she simply noted that this was something to work on.

One list led to another—"Important Things." She could think of the usual things: a home, money, love. What exactly love consisted of, or looked like, she was not quite sure but more was coming: trust, and, to be honest, approval. She liked making people happy. Was this good or bad? She didn't know, so she kept on writing, faster. She liked to dress well; she supposed she looked prim and proper in her dresses. Was this because of her mother? Was this to mask the decidedly un-prim part of her, the gay part? No, she liked to accentuate her waist, liked the classic look. It was comforting. Was this good or bad?

She wrote and wrote, her hand began to ache, the pen pushing into the callous bump on her middle finger. Arriving at the bottom of the page, she penned, "Michael Michael Michael Michael." That dear, sweet boy had made it all so simple.

Then Julia sat back and stared at her list.

When Jim returned to the drugstore counter, Mr. Wilderhausen leaned in to him and motioned with his head at the door Julia had just gone through. "I've seen love before, and that wasn't it."

"Doesn't matter to me, anyway," said Jim. "I got close enough to see she's not for me."

"You did, did you?" Mr. Wilderhausen nodded into his cup. "What did it—the beauty? The brains?"

Jim grabbed his jacket. "Later," he said, to no one in particular.

When he returned home, he charged through the door, the anger pent up inside him like an animal yanking on its chain. Miss Parnell had just stood there in the stairwell like an idiot, looking at Michael.

He wanted to tell the whole town: "It's true. Julia Parnell is a lesbian. Julia Parnell is a lesbian. Julia Parnell is a goddamned lesbian." He wanted to scream it from the police bullhorn. But he couldn't. Because he would look like a fool. Him!

He grabbed a beer from the fridge and popped it open, then sat at the kitchen table with paper and a pen that said "Wisconsin Dells." He cleared his throat and began:

Dear Principal Bob Ludlow,
It has come to my attention that a teacher under your
employment, Miss Julia Parnell, is a homosexual.

Jim used the formal version of the word, as he did with anyone
he didn't know very well.

I urge you to show caution where children are concerned.
Please investigate this matter discreetly and take appropri-
ate action. I will be in touch if I do not hear back from you
in a timely manner.
Sincerely,
Jim Clark, officer, Ackerman Police Department

He read over the letter and liked it, noting that he could sound as
schooled as any Harvard boy.

Eighteen

B y Saturday morning, Rose was at Julia's door, a duffel bag over her shoulder and a suitcase in her hand. She was flushed and out of breath, as if she'd run all the way from Iowa.

Julia clasped her hands at her mouth. "You came."

Rose nodded, and a sprig of chestnut curl dropped across her forehead, her dimples deepening with her smile. "I couldn't help it."

"Come in, come in," said Julia, grabbing the suitcase. "What did you tell work?"

"That I had a private matter to deal with. That I'd send stories from the road."

"How is Jane?"

"Julia, look at me." Rose cupped Julia's cheeks in her hands. "I missed you."

Julia saw that Rose's nose was growing pink, a sure sign she might cry. She kissed it, then said, "I was just about to make breakfast. Pancakes, your favorite."

Julia set the table for their first meal together in three months as Rose watched, leaning against the wall. She'd pulled her hair back in a bun, but unruly curls framed her face.

"We'll have canned cranberries at Thanksgiving. I won't even think of making the real thing," said Julia, trying to show Rose she hoped she'd stay at least a few weeks. Then she couldn't help herself: "You know, there's a small paper here, right in town. It covers the whole area. I'm sure they'd take you. I know my place is small, but

I think we could squeeze in here. If not, there are plenty of places around. I just saw a house for rent the other day. I've been thinking of getting out of here, anyway. Walking through that drug store to get to my own home is less than desirable."

"My, you're full of plans," said Rose.

Julia smiled at herself, silverware in hand. "I can't help it. I feel so . . . new. Like a different person. I know what to do now. I just want to *go*."

"Maybe we should think first."

"What do you mean, think? You mean you don't already know?"

"No. But we tried once and it didn't work. I need to know you've thought this through."

"I have. I made a list."

Rose laughed, and her cheeks shone. "And what did the list say?"

"All the things I did wrong last time and what I'm going to do differently."

Rose pursed her lips. "Your mother?"

"On the list."

"You've talked to her, then?"

Julia arranged the forks and knives. "Not yet. But I plan to. I said, it's on the list. I still have to figure out what to say."

"How about, 'I'm with Rose.' Or, if you want to be more specific, 'Rose is my girlfriend. I love Rose.'"

"She always knew. That's why she hated you."

"Still. You have to be able to say it."

"You lucked out with your parents. It isn't as easy for the rest of us."

"When is the last time you talked to her?"

Julia's mood was shifting. "About three weeks ago."

"That long? What did you talk about?"

"I know what you're getting at, Rose."

"Just answer. Let's talk this out."

Julia held up her hands. "I don't know. We talked about Penny from her bridge club. Her husband is cheating."

"And?"

"And whether she was going to hand out candy or nickels on Halloween."

"Did she ask if you were coming home to visit over the holidays?"

"No. She assumed . . . I told her I had plans."

"Did she wonder with whom?"

"No."

Rose stepped to the table and placed her hands on the back of the chair across from where Julia stood. "Did she ask about your job?"

"We didn't talk for very long."

"Your new home? Anything? Christ, Julia. You don't have a relationship with her, anyway. What are you afraid of?"

Julia was silent as she fingered a napkin she'd placed on the table.

"You do love me, don't you?" Rose asked.

"I do, hard as I try not to." Julia threw Rose a sheepish smile.

"Don't be charming," said Rose.

They stood in silence across the table from each other until Rose said, "If you love me, then, as Jane says, it's there to do. Might as well do it."

Julia glanced at Rose and stopped fussing with the table. She walked to the kitchen phone and picked up the receiver. After several seconds, Julia hung up and looked at Rose over the counter. "No answer."

"Next time, then."

From the moment Rose arrived, things seemed easier again, like summer in Iowa. The plaster cast had fully cracked, and it couldn't be refused. Not the same way. Julia could never go back to being that other person. She roamed the apartment in a glorious haze each day, fell asleep next to Rose like a happy child each night.

Out in the world, it was a bit harder. Each time they left the apartment, Julia snuck her list into her coat pocket in case she needed a glimpse while they were out, but even that made her feel foolish. How difficult was it to remember that love was an important thing, that Rose was dear to her? How disabled was she? Still, she carried the list.

Rose grabbed Julia's hand in the grocery store, and Julia flinched. Her hand grew moist, but she allowed Rose to hold on for a time. As they strolled the aisles, she perceived every glance from the shoppers pushing past with their grocery carts was a stare, a look pregnant with disbelief that two women were not only in love with each other, but would dare to display that love in public to the discomfort of those around them. They were making people sick. Julia prayed one of her student's parents would not appear. Or worse, Jim Clark.

Rose saw none of this or she ignored it. She was happily browsing the fruit when Julia saw a chance to disengage, and she let go of Rose's hand to reach for an apple, scouring it for bruises. Her other hand held tight to the paper in her pocket.

But when on the walk home Rose again laced her fingers into Julia's, Julia was a bit less afraid. And when they opened the drugstore door and walked through together, and Jim Clark was not there but Andy was, smiling, Julia felt like yet another bit of plaster had come off and floated away.

Just a few days later at school, a fellow teacher, probably thinking Julia had turned the corner, took out his handkerchief and wiped the water fountain clean after Julia drank from it. As she walked down the hallway back to her classroom, her throat burned. Could he possibly be worried he might get sick from her, believing those on the fringe who continued to claim the virus could be gotten by anybody, anyhow? Or maybe he just thought gay people were gross. Themselves a disease.

Then she caught herself. I can't take things personally, she reminded herself, it's not about me. She'd recited this every day for many days, but for the first time, she believed it. He was phobic of germs, she imagined, and wiped the water fountain every time he drank from it, along with doorknobs, car handles, and water faucets. He was a hermit living alone in a shiny clean germ-free house, and it was all because he'd once contracted a mysterious bacterial infection from a dirty public bathroom.

When she reentered her classroom, she told the children to stop cutting and gather around the beanbags for story time. She patted Michael's back when he sat next to her on the floor, and she couldn't remember ever feeling such content.

Nineteen

Tina had been absent at recess each day since she approached Michael in the shed, gone from the fence and also the playground. He didn't see her sitting on the monkey bars watching other children, or leaning against the brick wall of the school chewing her nails. Michael wondered vaguely where she was, what excuse she used to stay inside, but was relieved. He stayed in the classroom longer after school each day, talking with Miss Parnell, but there was no need. Tina was never there waiting when he opened the heavy front doors.

Miss Parnell had said it was not his fault he'd told Tina that she was gay, that it was actually a good thing. He didn't believe her at first, Mr. Clark had looked so angry in the stairwell, and she'd looked so sad. But now he did. Now he knew that Rose had come and Miss Parnell was happy.

"She would like to meet you," said Miss Parnell one day after school. "If that's alright."

They met Rose on their way from school to town. The air was cold, but the sun was bright and warmed Michael's cheeks. He was aware enough now to know that Miss Parnell and Rose were an odd couple, that two women in a relationship was different and weird and maybe wrong. He tried to make himself grossed out by it, but he wasn't. He looked at Rose as she smiled down at him with bright eyes and dimples, and he liked her.

"Let's just walk," said Rose. "It's too beautiful to go back inside."

Michael didn't mind answering Rose's questions about school and his mother and his farm in Minnesota. Something about the way Rose asked made him feel important, kind of how he felt with Miss Parnell. It made him happy they were together. When they turned a corner, Michael saw a police car idling at the curb across the street. He wondered if it was Mr. Clark, but the window was rolled up and all he could see was the reflection of tree branches. Something about the glass, though, made him feel watched, and he thought maybe he did see two dark holes staring out at him. Michael looked away then and tried to think of something else.

"What do you want to be when you grow up, Michael?" asked Rose.

No one had asked Michael this in a long time, and he hadn't thought about it since his father's death. Before that, he'd always assumed he would be a farmer. But how could he go back and get his farm now?

"I don't know," he said. "What can I do around here?"

"Why, anything you want."

"Maybe a baseball player."

Rose laughed. "Typical boy."

But Michael had only said that because he didn't know what else to say.

After awhile, he split from Rose and Miss Parnell and walked alone toward home. On the last block, he heard a car pull up alongside him. Mr. Clark rolled down the passenger-side window and called out.

"Where you going, Michael?"

"Home."

"Stop walking."

Michael looked over, surprised, but his legs kept moving.

"I said stop walking. Get in the car."

Michael focused on his house a half block away.

Mr. Clark stopped the police car and got out. Michael started to run, and Mr. Clark went after him, catching up quickly and grabbing Michael's arm. He whipped Michael around to face him.

"Listen to me, you little prick. If I tell you to stop, you stop."

Michael saw the gun at his hip and stared up into his black eyes and hoped that someone would look out their window and save him.

"What do you do with Miss Parnell every day?" asked Mr. Clark.

"Nothing."

"Don't lie to me. What do you do?"

"Nothing, we just hang out."

"I don't ever want to see you with her and her faggot friend again."

"You can't tell me what to do."

Mr. Clark dropped to his knee and spat moist breath at Michael's face. "It's not right. They're disgusting." He crumpled his nose and bared his teeth like a rodent. "You're disgusting."

"You're hurting my arm." Mr. Clark squeezed harder until his hand shook, and Michael winced. Then he let go and stood up. Michael turned and ran, past rows of quiet houses with blank windows staring out at him. He didn't dare look back, in fear Mr. Clark would come after him again. He threw open the door to his house and yelled for his mother. He ran into the kitchen, into her bedroom, but she wasn't there, wasn't anywhere. He ran back to the front door and bolted it but it didn't feel safe enough, so he checked each window, locked, locked, locked. He couldn't settle, so he moved from room to room until he found a spot that made him feel safe. He crawled to the back of his mother's closet, under her slacks and dresses, and sat, pulling his knees to his chest. By the time his mother came home an hour later, his breathing had calmed. Before she could find him, he crawled out, stood up, and went to greet her.

Julia sat facing Principal Ludlow, who was seated at his desk with his hands folded in front of him. He looked uncomfortable. Over in the corner, his secretary, Alice, typed notes.

Ludlow exhaled and looked at Julia over his bifocals. "We've got an issue, Julia, and there's no way around it. When the father of a local student, let alone a police officer, comes to me repeatedly, I've got to do something."

All Julia could think was, *Coward*.

"Jim Clark is an ugly, hateful man," she said.

"That might be so. But he's very upset. And he's not alone. Now that you've been all around town flaunting your—orientation—he's gotten to several other parents, and I've heard from each one. The private lives of the teachers at this school are expected to remain private, Julia."

Julia clenched her teeth. She felt like a swimmer in the middle of a lake with horseflies batting her head over and over. All she could do was duck under. But when she came up for air, they were still there.

"It shouldn't be an issue," she said.

Ludlow tapped his index finger on the top of his other hand. "Well, now it is."

"Why?"

"Because it is!"

Julia scooted forward in her seat. "Have you read the literature? We know how AIDS is transmitted, and it's not from being near a lesbian teacher."

Ludlow waved a hand. "That doesn't matter." He cleared his throat. "I understand you spend a good deal of time with Michael Nygaard?"

Julia sat back. "I have an agreement with his mother."

The two looked at each other in silence for several seconds. Ludlow was tapping his finger quickly now. "You've put me in a spot, Julia. Frankly, I don't know what to do yet, but we're going to do something." He searched among his papers until he found the one he was looking for. "I had Alice type up a list of questions to consider," he said, scanning the document. "You can help me right now with some of them. For instance, how will you handle this with your students if and when they ask?"

Shame began to creep in around the edges. How easily it showed back up. Julia's hand smoothed her hair, slowly rounded her ear. "I don't think that will happen."

"You're fooling yourself. You need to think about it. We should probably talk with parents, too. Put them at ease."

"I don't think that's necessary."

Ludlow set down the paper and took off his glasses. "If you're going to live openly, you'll need to live with the consequences. Parents have to feel comfortable with you as their children's teacher."

Julia was silent. Ludlow waited for an answer.

"I'm just thinking," said Julia. "I'm wondering whether you've ever talked with parents about your relationship with your wife."

"Julia."

"It's a fair question."

"You're making an unfair comparison. Apples and oranges."

"Which fruit is the pedophile?"

"Oh, come on."

"At least be honest. That's what's at issue here, isn't it? Otherwise, why would you care? Or is it just good old-fashioned prejudice?"

Ludlow frowned. "I like you, Julia. But there is nothing in our anti-discrimination policy that prohibits me from letting you go if I feel this puts an undue burden on the students or their parents."

"Undue burden?"

"Or if I feel it interferes with your teaching."

"All I want to do is teach."

"Good," he said. "Then it's settled. I'll be in touch."

The next day, Julia stood at the front of the classroom looking down at her students, their feet kicking under desks, hands rubbing noses, some whispering, others staring out the window. Michael flipped through the pages of his *National Geographic*, and she felt an ache because she knew that from now on their relationship would be different.

She held her grade book, paper-clipped to the month of November. It was almost Thanksgiving break, time to collect overdue homework, total up points, and make sure all was in order for December. She stuck her finger in the book at the paperclip and flipped it open. Written across the two pages, in black marker, was the word, "HOMO."

She looked at the word for a long while, trying to remember how she should think and what she should do, but she felt washed over, thoughts spinning in her mind like a body in a tidal wave. She heard Jenny ask, "Miss Parnell, are you okay?"

Julia didn't answer right away. She tried to quiet her mind and open her mouth and finally said, "Robin, you have forty-seven points for November. Paul, I still need last week's spelling homework."

That was how she got through the day—line by line. Talking about what she knew for sure, what was written down right before her eyes, skipping over the thick black interruptions from the word across the pages.

Later, she didn't tell Rose about the word because then she'd have to have a reaction that pleased her. Try as she might, she couldn't grasp and hold the feeling she'd had that day in the reading circle.

Julia would be required to write a letter to the parents of her students, discussing her relationship in the most discreet manner (Ludlow's term) and assuring them that it would not be a topic of discussion in the classroom. Should any students ask, she would simply say it was a private matter.

On her dining room table, Julia arranged a stack of typed letters, envelopes, stamps, the school address book, and a pen. Then she sat and folded her hands, looking out across the items.

"I can't do it," she finally said.

"Then don't," said Rose, who was reading on the couch. "Just because you're gay doesn't mean you have to send a newsletter."

"That's what it means to my boss."

"What does it mean to you?"

Julia sighed. "Does it matter? I need to work."

"Of course it matters. You can't live your life for other people."

"You've always had a knack for clichés."

"Why do you think they're clichés, Julia?" Rose closed her book and walked past Julia into the bedroom. "I'm taking a nap," she said, and she closed the door but then came back out. She stood next to Julia and stroked her hair until Julia looked up at her.

"I want you to be happy," said Rose. "I don't know how to help you."

"Why do you think I need help?"

Rose didn't know how to answer, to put into words what came to mind—a woman standing on a wooden ladder full of wormholes—and be loving at the same time.

"Do you remember," she asked, "when we were little, the school nurse would come into the classroom and call each child up to the front of the room one by one and check for lice? We always knew who had them because she'd send the child out of the room to sit and wait in her office. And remember one year Timmy Urban, who was so poor he wore his sister's hand-me-down shirts, was told to go to the nurse's office, and he cried from embarrassment? This was a boy who used to call you Julia Poopnell. But the moment you saw his tears, you decided the way the nurse was doing it was wrong. And you told her so. Then you told Mrs. Maxwell, and the principal, and even your parents. And you kept it up until they changed it. From then on, we stood in a line outside the nurse's office and went in one by one."

"I was seven. It was easy."

"You were concerned about people being humiliated."

"Yes."

"The point is, you have to have the same care for yourself. Do you think what is happening to you is right?"

"Nothing's happening to me. I wasn't fired."

"No, but you might as well have been. They're probably hoping you'll leave. Mr. Clark wants to run you out of town. Is that right?"

"Of course not."

"Then say so."

"It's not that easy."

"Why?"

"Because this isn't second grade, Rose."

"No, it's not. But you knew what was right back then, and you didn't care what anyone else thought."

"I'm the one with lice this time."

"That's my point. You have to be willing to stick up for yourself as much as you stuck up for Timmy Urban. Remember when I got pregnant in high school?"

"I don't need all these sappy stories," said Julia.

"Yes, you do. I was ashamed, but you wouldn't let me think I was shameful," said Rose. "You were fierce. You don't seem as fierce anymore."

"That was easy," said Julia. "It was easy to stand by you."

"Because it was secret."

Julia thought. Was that it? Partly. But no. "Isn't it always easier to be the calm one when someone is upset? To be the brave one when someone else isn't? Now you're the brave one. And I don't know what to do."

Rose sat on Julia's lap and put her arms around her, hugging Julia's head to her chest. Her hair was so soft, so shiny, it had always reminded Rose more of liquid than hair. "I think," said Rose, "that's because you haven't yet figured out what *you* are. You react to me, to everyone else."

"I came here on my own, didn't I?"

"Because of the people back in Iowa. What do *you* want?"

Julia hated this question. She wanted to change herself. "I want to feel happy," she said. "I want to be okay with being a lesbian. I don't want to care what people think of me."

"You can do that," said Rose. "It will take practice. A lot of it."

Julia tried again. She tried every moment for days. Being gay, being out, began to define her to such an extent that every smile directed her way made her think, *That's nice. There's someone who isn't prejudiced.* She began stopping her car at crosswalks, even if there was not a stop sign. She waved others to go before her, gave up her place in the grocery line to elderly women, left large tips at the drugstore counter. These niceties were an apology to anyone she offended. She would be so nice they would forget she was gay.

She perceived slights where there weren't any. When Andy didn't see her on her way out, he looked away on purpose. When a colleague asked her a question in the hallway, he had to force himself to talk to her so as not to be deemed prejudiced. And when in the middle of all this Anne sent her a photo she'd taken of Julia with Michael outside their home, Julia became Anne's token gay friend. *How lovely,* she thought, *that she can use me to feel better about herself.*

But the worst was the way she now felt with her students. When they smiled at her, she pursed her lips back in a curt manner. She thought twice about placing her hand on Jenny's shoulder as she commended her on her paper, and didn't. To avoid being accused of favoring girls, she gave Sophia a B+ though the girl deserved an A and overwhelmingly called on the boys who raised their hands— except Michael. She spoke less, careful with every word or turn of a phrase that might be interpreted the wrong way. She even wondered if the school had placed a hidden camera in her classroom.

It felt interminable. And she hadn't even written the letters yet. She imagined the whole town going to their mailboxes, finding a note from her, calling the family around the table to read it together, gasping, giggling, smirking. People might be kind on the outside, she thought, but often it was just the facade they put up to cover who they really were.

"You're losing yourself," Rose told her.

Twenty

For several days, Miss Parnell was not available to talk at recess or after school. Michael knew something was different. She still looked at him with something like affection, but a part was missing. He knew she'd gotten into trouble with the principal, and that people were talking about her. His mother said that Miss Parnell was going through a difficult time right now, and he should give her space if she wanted it. So he waited for her to ask him to stay inside at recess or go for ice cream. But she didn't.

Instead, she called Anne.

"Please let Michael know none of this is his fault," said Julia over the phone. "It's just, there are so many eyes on me right now."

"Of course," said Anne. "I understand. We understand."

So Michael went to the tavern each day after school. Anne prepared his snack of apples, crackers, and milk, which he ate at a corner table surrounded by homework and magazines. When it got busy, he moved to the prep area and read between mounds of onions and celery or watched Cesar, the cook, chop chickens into pieces so fast Michael waited to see if a finger got lopped off and thrown into the bowl of meat. Once in a while, a drop of sweat fell from Cesar's forehead onto the cutting board, or into the food, and Michael would lose sight of it as Cesar worked.

None of the waitresses, cooks, or busboys said anything about Michael coming in and taking up space, or taking Anne's attention away in moments. Her brother said nothing about the apples and milk taken from the refrigerator and even, it seemed to Anne, stocked the refrigerator with more. It reminded her of Kevin as a little boy.

One afternoon, Anne walked downstairs to grab more olives for Chip, who had complained his garnish tray was empty. It was a Friday, so many early drinkers were already there, including Joe, and the bar area was full.

She found Nancy walking out of the office, stuffing dollar bills into her apron pocket. She was slightly startled by Anne.

Normally, Anne might not want to get involved. But this was her brother's business.

"What were you doing?" she asked.

Nancy looked at her straight on. "Getting money."

"For what? From where?"

"For Joe. From the safe."

"How dare you."

"Kevin knows. He's the one who gave me the combination."

"Why?"

"So Joe can pay for his drinks."

Anne pursed her lips. "Why not tell Chip to put it on the house?"

"He doesn't want anyone to know."

"Why? It's his restaurant."

"Kevin doesn't want to humiliate Joe. Plus, then everyone'll want a freebie."

"So that's why the drawers are off."

"Just a few dollars here and there." Nancy smiled. "We like watching Chip freak out. Kevin slips Joe more from his own pocket, when he's here."

"How long have you been doing this?"

"A few months. Since he was laid off from the community college. Smartest guy I've ever heard talk, if you can get him going. He's got no family. I asked Kevin if he'd help. You know, let him keep one thing in his life. He's been a regular for years."

"Maybe drinking is why he lost his job."

Nancy shrugged. "Who are we to say?"

"But we could actually help him."

"I think we are."

They stood facing each other across the empty prep table. Anne moved to get the olives on the shelf behind Nancy.

"He's old, Anne," said Nancy over her shoulder. "Too old to quit."

Anne came back to the table and set the jar down. "I think it's nice what you and Kevin are doing."

Nancy remained at the table, made no move to head upstairs. "Joe scares the hell out of me, you know?" she said. "He had this great life, and now he just has the bar every day. I just keep thinking, he's someone's son. Someone cared for him. He was a boy once, and his mother had such high hopes."

Anne considered Nancy for a moment, confused by her words, and then it came to her. "You have a child," she said.

Nancy nodded. "He's in fourth grade over at the elementary school."

Anne's eyebrows raised. "Same as Michael," she said. "I wonder why I didn't know that."

"You never asked."

Nancy walked back upstairs, and Anne stood at the empty prep table with her hands in her apron pocket. She and Nancy both had sons the same age. She smiled to herself as she realized that both she and Nancy were also single mothers. They were both career waitresses. Her smile turned into a giggle and her shoulders shook as she brought a hand up to stifle the laugh erupting from her mouth. She'd never stopped to consider that she was one of them.

Later, Kevin stopped by the tavern before he left for the weekend. Anne approached him in the office and stood opposite where he sat at his desk.

"Where are you off to this time?" she asked.

"Oh, the usual." He rifled through the papers scattered on the desk. "Have you seen the checkbook?"

Anne shook her head. She'd never seen the checkbook.

"Ah, found it." Kevin signed the top check and moved to the next.

"I know about Joe," said Anne.

Kevin looked up for a moment, then resumed signing. "Yeah, well."

"I think it's nice. Though I admit, I was a little jealous when Nancy told me."

"Jealous?"

"It reminded me how little I know about your life. You and I used to be good friends. You used to do little things like that for me."

"That was before you got married and started your own family."

"I remember that it was before you left the state," said Anne, a bit too curt.

Kevin paused his work and looked at Anne, confused. "All I meant is that it was before we grew up."

"So you admit you've changed."

"What do you mean?"

Anne closed the office door. "You're different. You're removed."

"Removed? I'm sorry, Anne, that I can't run around the neighborhood with you anymore."

"You hardly smile. You have this wall around you. You barely even came to the funeral." Anne could see herself standing before Kevin, emoting, and felt a vague foolishness. She hadn't planned this outpouring, wouldn't have wanted to, but found the words spilling out before her thoughts could stop them. "And why haven't you asked Michael to go fishing yet? The boy has no father! He wants to go with you. You're here, in the same town, and you never see him!"

"What about you? Have you gone fishing with him?"

"We've never even been to your house. Where do you live? I don't even know!"

Kevin looked back down at his desk and grabbed his pen.

Anne clenched her teeth. "What changed? I'm your sister. Why haven't you asked us over? You have an enormous house all to yourself. Are you too good now, too good for farmers' wives and pickup trucks? Is that it? That's not you, Kevin!" He ignored her. Anne put her hands on the desk and leaned over. "That's not where we came from."

"No. That's not it."

"Then what? What's wrong with you? You used to tell me everything. Why don't I even know where you live?"

"Because I'm embarrassed." He tossed his pen onto his desk. "I'm embarrassed, Anne."

She straightened for a moment and then sat in the chair across from her brother.

"I don't understand."

Kevin leaned back and rubbed his face with both hands, turning his cheeks and nose red, before he spoke. "A few years ago, I met a woman. She manages the restaurant in St. Louis. After awhile— too long—I found out she was married. But she told me she wasn't happy. She told me they were getting a divorce, that they'd already called the lawyers. That she chose me. We continued seeing each other. I flew down there every weekend. I asked her to move up here with me and she said yes. So I built the house."

"And she never came."

Kevin shook his head. "She never came."

"So sell it."

Kevin looked at Anne, deciding how to continue. "I still see her. I still fly down every weekend."

Anne raised her eyebrows. "Does her husband know?"

"Yes. They're—separated, or whatever. I don't even know for sure." He put his head in his hands. "It's so messed up, Anne."

She looked at the top of his head, unsure what to say, twisting her apron in her lap. "Oh, I don't know. Who's to say what's normal."

"Don't bother."

"Well, it's true, really. Right now I feel I'd do just about anything to have John back."

He considered her for a moment, his brown eyes watching until she cocked her head in suspicion. "What?" she asked.

"You could always say the thing that made me feel better. Made me feel normal."

"Really? I remember always feeling helpless. You were so good to me, and I never felt I clearly showed you the same."

He shook his head. "No. That's one of the reasons I left—to be on my own. To prove to myself that I didn't need you to protect me."

"To me you were always that independent. Always going off, leading the way. Always happy. It never seemed to bother you, all the teasing."

"Anne, of course it bothered me. I was a kid. That's a ridiculous thing to say."

"I suppose you're right. My God—it is. It is ridiculous."

He waved her off. "Never mind."

"Is that where you're going now—to see her?"

He nodded and looked away, past Anne.

"It will work itself out," she said.

"I've thought for a while that it might not. Believe me, I've waited. I've perfected simply enduring. Sometimes I can step back and see myself, and I think, My God, just *do* something."

"Moving out of that big house doesn't mean you failed at anything. It just means an idea ended."

He smiled and inhaled deeply, and Anne thought she saw tears forming. "See?" he said. "Still dependent on your wisdom."

She brought a hand to her cheek. "Oh my, if that's the truth then you're in for it."

Jim had waited what he considered a decent amount of time. He'd laid off Ludlow awhile now, and then when he finally called again, he discovered that Ludlow was not going to fire Miss Parnell. Ludlow said Jim should feel good about the damn letter, that this was an appropriate solution. But not to Jim, it wasn't. Not even close.

He stood in his uniform in front of the open refrigerator, growing angrier with each slice of ham he peeled out of a deli bag. Cassie had taken Tina to the McDonald's drive-thru to pick up cheeseburgers for dinner. Over on a kitchen chair, folded laundry sat stacked in a basket. Jim's eyes stopped on the top shirt, which had "Minnesota" written across an outline of the state. He walked over to the basket and picked up the shirt, definitely not Tina's. Though he had an idea who it belonged to.

"Who's is this?" he asked Cassie when they returned. He held up the shirt.

Cassie looked over at Tina, who sat looking at the food bag she'd placed on the table, then said, "Michael Nygaard's."

"What is Mike's shirt doing in Tina's laundry?"

Cassie waved him away. "Oh, I just said I'd do it for him."

"Why? Why would you be washing Michael's shirt?"

Cassie walked up to Jim and put her hand on his chest. "It's no biggie."

"I said, why would a boy be leaving his shirt here, in my daughter's house?"

Cassie shrugged. "She just came home wearing it one day."

He grabbed Cassie's wrist and pushed her away from him, turning toward Tina.

"Tell me."

"What?"

"Tell me!"

She told him.

Jim strode across the street, still wearing his uniform, and pounded on the Nygaards' door. Anne opened it.

"What kind of boy are you raising?" he asked between his teeth.

"Excuse me?"

"This was in my daughter's laundry," he said, showing her

Michael's T-shirt balled up in his fist. "Why, I asked her, would she have a boy's T-shirt? Well? Do you know why?" His chest heaved.

Anne shook her head.

"Because Michael made advances on her in your shed." Jim tossed the shirt to Anne.

She caught it against her chest. "You're mistaken."

"No," he shook his head emphatically. "No, no. Michael took off his shirt and talked Tina into taking off hers." He lowered his voice and bared his teeth. "Then he tried to *touch* her."

Anne was unfazed. "Michael would never do that."

"Ask him." He shifted from one foot to another.

"You need to leave."

"No."

"I'll speak with Michael and talk to you about this later."

"I'm not going anywhere. Ask him."

She called Michael to the door and put her arm around his shoulders. "Did Tina take her shirt off in the shed?"

"You talked her into it," Jim said.

"No," protested Michael. "That's not true. She just took it off."

"Why would she do that?" asked Jim.

"She said it was hot."

Jim snickered, spittle forming at the corner of his mouth. "God, boys are starting younger and younger."

"That's enough," said Anne. "Michael said he didn't do it. He doesn't lie."

"Neither does my daughter."

"Then I'm afraid we're at an impasse, and we'll have to chalk it up to a misunderstanding."

Jim looked at Anne and spat his words. "If you don't have the time to watch your child, then maybe you shouldn't have any."

Anne patted Michael's back. "Go check on supper." He did as his mother asked, and Anne turned back to Jim. "I think you need to ask your daughter how she happened to just *let* a boy, a younger boy, talk her into taking her shirt off. You might also ask her why she comes searching for supper at our house. Now go home. And don't ever talk to me like that in front of my child again."

She moved to close the door, but Jim put his hand up against it.

"Tina was his only friend, you know," he said. "The kid sits under a damn tree by himself every day because all the kids make fun of him. And this is how he repays her."

Anne closed the door, but the words were already inside, and she leaned with them against the wall.

All the kids? She hadn't known, or had she, that he was alone. Some trouble with the other boys, Miss Parnell had told her, just general enough that Anne could fool herself. She couldn't listen, couldn't hold it. When was that? Weeks ago. Weeks.

It was the image of her son sitting under the tree that startled her heart. Why didn't she know the details? He went to school every day to face it, and she sent him off, unaware. Unaware on purpose. How could she?

Walking down the hall toward the kitchen, she could see Michael pulling the tenderloin out of the oven, the mitts almost reaching his elbows. The issues surrounding her little boy were as complex as a knot of necklaces, and she was unsure what she could say to untangle them.

She sat at the kitchen table and watched her son step about the kitchen, opening cupboards and shutting drawers. Preparing for her—offering, wanting nothing. This dear boy with the weight of the world on his shoulders. Anne's tears came quietly at first, but soon they streamed so capaciously, Michael stopped working and looked at her.

"Let's go outside," she said, and once they were standing on the prickly grass of the backyard, she looked up at the silver maple in the corner. She closed her eyes and imagined pines.

"I haven't done this right," she said, the tears licking her lips. "You might think that because I'm the adult, I know what to do all the time. It's not true. I've fumbled this. I was struck just as hard by your father's death as you were, and I didn't know how to lead you through it. I didn't know how to lead myself through it. I said we had to bear down, but that's all we've been doing. We've had our heads down, siding up to it, walking around it, letting it hang there in the middle. We've had our heads down so we can't see where we're going. I didn't realize we can go straight through with our heads up. I've focused on making a living, but I fooled myself into thinking that was all I had to do. I'm sorry. I'm sorry, Michael, for not paying attention."

Michael was confused at first, watching his mother's sudden show of emotion. Then a small spark of relief started deep in the dark of his body. But he didn't tell his mother it was okay.

"I imagine you're angry," she said. "I would be." She watched his young eyes, could see how easy it was to find happiness in them, to bypass the sadness. "Michael, I don't even know whether you've grieved. Have you cried?"

He supposed he hadn't, not really. There hadn't been actual tears for a long time, but his insides always felt like they were crying. He didn't know whether that counted.

"Why didn't you tell me about the kids at school?" she asked.

Michael was quiet. He didn't want his mother to know, but he did. So much. He wanted her to ask again.

"You didn't want to bother me?" she asked.

Michael was reluctant, could not push the words up from his belly, where they lay in a mire. He felt sick.

Still, Anne tried another way. "Why won't they talk to you?"

"Because I'm adopted," he said finally, and he kicked at the turf with the toe of his shoe. "Being adopted is not good, Mom." His tears fell, and his voice strained. "I thought if I told you, you'd be embarrassed." He didn't cover his face with his hands, didn't put his chin down to his chest. He cried to his mother, his mouth wrenched with sorrow.

Anne had no words. She cupped his face for a moment and then pulled him down and onto her lap. "No," she said. "No way. Not ever." They sat in the grass, her arms and back curving around him like the earth.

Michael cried and cried. And she let him. She held him and she let him. She didn't try to calm him, didn't say, "There, there," or "It's okay." She didn't try to explain it. She just let him be.

He cried for a long time. And then he stopped. The sadness remained, but he could carry it, spread over the fullness of his body, in the arms of his mother. It didn't feel, as it had for months, like it was about to explode from his chest or his gut or his head.

"The grief festered too long," said Anne. She wiped his cheeks with her thumb. "Your father cried sometimes, you know."

"I know. I saw him once."

"You did?"

"The time he took me to watch the wolves. I don't think he was sad, though. We were just sitting there, talking."

Anne flinched. That was less than a year ago.

"He cried when we brought you home, too. He cried a whole bunch that day." She rested her cheek on Michael's head and stroked his chin. "It's going to be hard, doing the rest of your growing without a father."

"I can still picture him. I can still hear what he would say. Sometimes it's like he's standing in the room. I have to write it all down so I don't forget."

Anne knew that even so, the clarity would go away. John would become a story, something almost indiscernible from real memory. But maybe all memories were like that. She ached for her husband, for the truth that Michael wouldn't know him well. "I can't take the place of a father for you," she said. "But I can do a lot. We have to remain close, we have to talk. I promise I'll do better."

They sat together through the dinner hour, into the evening, onto the night, as the tenderloin grew cold in the kitchen and the stars peeked out. Then, Anne and Michael noticed the giant maple looked beautiful, black against a sapphire sky.

Michael felt more loved than he had in a long time. He felt something like his normal self, the one from Minnesota. But new.

Twenty-One

Michael and his father waited in the clearing for half an hour more for the omega to return. But they saw no sign of him.

"Maybe he's in a trap," said Michael.

"Maybe. Let's go back a different way and look for more."

The path wound around the other side of the hill, near farms Michael had never seen. They were several miles north of home.

"Do the wolves ever see you?" asked Michael.

"I think wolves see everything."

"Why don't they attack you?"

"They're not aggressive," said John. "Not toward people, anyway." They crunched along on the frozen earth, leaving a field and entering the woods. "Are you cold?"

"Yes," said Michael. "No."

John stopped. "Here, take my scarf." He wrapped the wool around Michael's neck and head. "Just a few more miles. It'll be lunch by the time we get back."

"Soup," said Michael.

"Hot chocolate," said his father. "But you know, I never minded the cold very much. One of my fondest memories takes place in the cold."

"What?"

"It was the middle of December. Your mother sat atop a haystack as I pitched hay off the wagon to the cows. It was cold, the sky black except for a thousand white stars. It was peaceful. Quiet."

Father and son exited the trees and stood on the shores of a frozen lake, discernible only by the dip in the sheath of snow. In the middle stood a gray wolf.

It watched them, having been alerted by their movement several moments before they stepped out from the trees. Michael and his father stood motionless.

"They did it," said John. "They drove him out."

Even from a distance, the wolf looked impressive. He stood taut, ears perked, his tail straight back. He belonged here, part of the landscape, as natural a form as the pine trees behind him.

"Will he die?" asked Michael.

John picked at his eyebrow. "He'll have to watch out for other wolves. He'll have a hard time hunting. He's lucky it's almost spring, though the odds aren't with him."

Michael stared at the wolf and could not blink even against the chilly wind or the snow pellets that continued to swirl. The wolf kept his gaze, and Michael saw something familiar, or felt it, in those amber eyes staring. What started as alertness softened. The wolf blinked once, then sniffed the snow before looking back. He turned away and trotted off, kicking up bits of snow and leaving a path behind him. Michael watched as the wolf reached the woods on the other side of the lake and disappeared without looking back.

"But sometimes," said his father, "the wolf forms his own pack. He becomes the alpha." John was still looking at the trees where the wolf disappeared. "He knows what he has to do to survive, and he does it."

Michael suddenly felt tired. Tired of watching the other children play. Tired, even, of flipping through his magazine and the books he brought out from the library. He had stayed under his tree for many weeks, and he felt stiff. Like he needed to move. So he stood up.

Nancy's son was named Sam.

Michael walked back across the field toward the school, his hands stuffed in his coat pockets. Circles of girls in tights and winter coats dotted the grass, and he instinctively went to one of them. Girls usually knew what was what.

"Do any of you know Sam?" asked Michael, willing himself not to sound nervous, not to be nervous. "He's a fourth grader in Mrs. O'Neil's class."

"Sure," said a girl with a pink plastic headband in her hair. She pointed to the monkey bars. "He's over there in the orange jacket."

"Thanks," he said. That was easy.

He walked toward the playground and for the first time didn't feel afraid. He watched Jason and his friends at the tetherball. As Michael neared, Jason grabbed the ball and pounded it with his fist at him. Still, Michael walked closer, glancing beyond Jason to the farther side of the playground and the monkey bars where Sam had linked his feet and was hanging upside down. Looking back to Jason, he watched indifferently as Jason pounded the ball again and again, with each of Michael's steps. But Michael's legs moved with the confidence he used to show on the baseball field, and Jason stayed put. He glared, but he stayed put. Whatever Jason wanted, Michael wasn't giving him.

Michael began to smile, tried to bite his lip. When he walked past Jason, he full-out grinned. He heard Jason yell, "Retard!" but he had already walked past and was looking ahead toward Sam.

When Michael reached him, his face was very red and sweaty, his blonde hair falling in spikes toward the ground.

"Hey," said Michael. "I think our moms work together."

"At Murphy's?" asked Sam.

"Yeah. Your mom is Nancy, right?"

"Uh huh."

"Do you ever go in after school?" asked Michael.

"Sometimes, but mostly I go to a sitter's." Sam started swinging. His face looked as though it was about to explode. "Wanna come up?" he asked.

Michael climbed to the top of the bars, hooked his feet, and fell backward.

"I'm Michael," he said.

"I'm Sam." He stopped swinging. "Wait until all the blood rushes to your head. You'll get a huge headache."

Michael waited, and his head felt heavy and full, so full the smile on his face barely had room.

On the day before Thanksgiving break, Tina appeared at the fence during recess, but Michael wasn't there. That meant he was inside with Miss Parnell, so she turned back to her own playground but then caught sight of him walking up and over the rainbow bars. She held on to the chain links above her head and watched as he and another boy took turns racing across, stepping gingerly with each foot on the narrow rings. She wore a T-shirt, impervious to the cold, though goose bumps rose from her skinny arms.

After a few moments, she called to him. He glanced but continued his game.

"Michael!" she said again. He walked over, but she couldn't tell if he was angry or not. He looked—indifferent.

"I know you don't want to talk to me," said Tina when he arrived at the fence.

Michael started to shrug, to brush it off, but said, "No, I don't," and he looked back to the playground.

"I was a total bitch," she said, airily. "I can't help it sometimes."

He faced her. "That's stupid."

Tina's eyebrows narrowed. "What's that supposed to mean?"

"You can help it. You just don't."

A small gasp of air left her throat in something like a chuckle. "No, I can't."

"Give me a break."

Tina was at a loss. "Give *me* a break. What's gotten into you, anyway?"

Michael shrugged. "I'm sick of it."

Tina's voice raised a few notes. "Of what?"

"You're nice, then you're mean. You're nice, then you're mean. It's hard to be friends with you."

"How would you know?" she said. "You don't have any other friends except Miss Parnell."

She looked for any sign that Michael was hurt by her words, but she saw none. He looked like he was just standing in line at the end of the school day, waiting to leave. She wanted to dive through one of the fence holes and stand next to him. He inhaled and looked like he might walk away.

"I didn't move here last spring," she said. "We moved here three years ago."

He watched her.

"I felt stupid."

"About what?"

"I don't have any friends, either. Like you."

Michael considered this. "You don't have to lie," he said. "To be friends. You don't have to lie."

Tina fingered a jelly bracelet on her wrist, twisting it around an index finger until it squeezed her wrist too tight.

"Do you even like me?" asked Michael. "I mean, in the shed. Do you like me that way?"

Tina snorted. "No. You're like my brother."

"Then why did you do that?"

Tina threw her hands in the air. "I don't know. I thought I could get you to like me."

"You don't have to do that, either, to be friends," he said. "It's weird."

Somehow Tina was beginning to feel lighter. Her green eyes caught the sun and glistened.

"I'm never coming over to your house," said Michael.

Tina nodded.

"And don't make fun of me anymore."

They fell into an understanding from then on. They were neighborhood buddies, thrust together by proximity. Like siblings, as Tina said, more than anything else. Tina showed up for dinner often and no one treated her like company. They played tag or rode bikes on weekends. The two were different, though, and without saying it or even realizing it, they knew the differences were important.

That fall, a strange thing happened. Indian summer came twice. Everyone had bowed their heads against the coming winter when the breeze changed in the middle of a Wednesday. It was warm, brown and warm, unlike spring's sharp light green. Wet brown branches like sponges soaked against the gray sky. People walked outside in short sleeves amid the barren trees and yellowed grass and talked about how they couldn't ever remember it being so mild this late in November.

The afternoon before Thanksgiving felt like a party. It was the start of a four-day break from school and work. Firecrackers, left over from the previous summer, exploded intermittently in the early darkening sky. The air smelled like rain that might come, fresh and promising. Even the crickets were making noise, rubbing the humid air between their legs, pulled out of hibernation by the heat. It was the kind of afternoon you wanted to walk into and wrap your arms around.

Michael and Sam passed Westway Drugs on their way to Murphy's after school. They looked through the open door to see men sitting at the counter scratching Lotto tickets, smoking cigarettes, and drinking Cokes in red plastic cups. Mr. Wilderhausen blew his nose in his handkerchief, turning away from the counter and waving at them with one hand while he wiped with his other. Michael saw Mr. Clark inside, and the men laughed at something he said.

On the sidewalk, Miss Parnell walked up holding a bag of groceries. She smiled, and Michael thought maybe it was like the old smile.

"Michael, how nice to see you," she said. "What a lovely day to be out walking." She looked to Sam and extended her hand. "I'm Miss Parnell."

"This is Sam," said Michael. "We're going to get our mothers, and then we're going for ice cream."

"Ice cream in November. Isn't this the strangest weather?"

"Want to come?"

"Oh, thank you," she said. "I would love to, but I have to start dinner."

"My mom won't mind. She said you're welcome any time. She doesn't care what anybody says. I don't, either."

Michael was glad he said it, would always be glad he said it, but Miss Parnell looked uncomfortable and she switched her grocery bag to her other arm. "Thank you. Maybe another time. Soon."

But then she didn't walk away. Instead, she set down her bag of groceries and crouched on the sidewalk, looking up at him. "I hope you have a lovely Thanksgiving," she said. "A lovely—everything."

Michael nodded. He thought she might hug him because she looked at him so long, but she kept her hands in her lap.

He watched as Miss Parnell walked away, her shiny blonde hair swaying with the movement. She turned left into Westway Drugs and disappeared into the smoke. Michael heard one of the men inside say, "Such a waste." The words gave Michael shivers for some reason, and he wanted to run back to his teacher. But that would be silly, so he continued down the street, away from her.

Twenty-Two

The chicken Julia bought burned in the oven. She couldn't concentrate on anything; could only think how to tell Rose that she'd decided go back to Kansas. That Rose had come for nothing. That Julia was a disappointment.

"Let's boil some pasta," she said, and she dropped the chicken into the garbage.

She lit candles, and they talked as they ate. Julia grew comfortable in the mundane conversation.

"Any chance you have coffee?" asked Rose when they finished and carried their plates to the sink.

Julia shook her head. "Just tea."

"The drugstore, then." Rose saw the look on Julia's face. "It'll be fine. It's getting late. Maybe he's gone home."

"It's a holiday. He'll still be there."

But when Rose peeked in, she grabbed Julia's hand and pulled her through the door. "Coast is clear."

A few men were at the far end of the counter. Mr. Wilderhausen sat reading the newspaper. He nodded at Julia and Rose as they sat at the other end.

"Coffee, please," said Rose to Andy.

"Sure thing." He turned to Julia. "Tea no milk?"

"Thank you."

Andy turned and grabbed the hot water pot that now stayed out on the back counter by the coffee machine. As he prepared their drinks, the door opened, and Jim Clark walked in with Steve Lubbock, fresh from the liquor store, each holding a small paper bag. Julia stiffened, and Rose put a hand on her arm.

"Don't let him make you leave. I'm right here. We'll just talk."

Rose looked over at the men and made eye contact with Jim Clark. There was no mistaking the disdain in his eyes. Rose thought he rather looked like the caricature of a villain in some movie, beady little eyes, and almost laughed.

"How can you be so relaxed?" asked Julia.

Rose was taken aback. "I don't know. People like him, you just have to have a sense of humor."

"But you know I'm upset. Doesn't that matter to you?"

"Of course. I'm sorry."

But Julia was ready for a fight. "If you cared about how I felt, about how hard this is for me, you wouldn't be able to make light of it."

"That's not true."

"It is true. You think everyone should be like you. You can't imagine how others feel."

A roar of laughter came from the men around Jim Clark. And Jim's voice grew louder: "What's the definition of confusion? . . . Three blind lesbians in a fish market." More laughter.

Rose glanced that way but threw her eyes right back to Julia. They could still hear the conversation down the counter.

"She seems like a nice enough lady," said Mr. Wilderhausen, who at least seemed to be trying to talk quietly, his back to Julia.

"She fucks women, Bob," said Jim. "It doesn't matter if she's nice."

"Hey, you're the one who dated a lesbian." Mr. Wilderhausen's shoulders heaved up and down, stifling the laughter inside him.

"I didn't date her," said Jim.

"Oh, no? You made such a stink about it. Are you telling us you made it up?" He feigned surprise.

Jim was silent and Steve chimed in. "Wait—so you were just outed by a lesbian? Classic."

Julia shook her head. "I can't."

Rose placed a hand on Julia's knee. "You can."

Andy returned with their cups and set them down, looking briefly at Jim, but said only, "Enjoy, ladies," then returned to his crossword puzzle midway down the counter.

"Here's one," said Steve. "What did one lesbian say to another? . . . Your face or mine?"

"Maybe you don't actually love me," said Julia.

Rose snorted. "You're joking."

"What's the difference between a bowling ball and a lesbian?"

"Alright, cut it out," Andy said.

"You wouldn't push me so much," said Julia. "You would support me."

"Don't put this on me," said Rose.

The laughter died as the two women stood up.

"See you," said Andy. He looked apologetic, and Julia felt bad, then annoyed. What good does an apologetic smile do? Why couldn't he just say something? Rose was already at the door, but Julia paused, her hand still resting on her stool. The voices in the background started up again, the men laughing. One voice over another, they talked now of Thanksgiving turkey and gizzards. They echoed in Julia's head like pebbles in an empty tin can. Clank. Clinkety. Clank. Over and over and over. She was going to leave this town, leave it behind. Kick up dust in their faces. Gone.

She became aware that the voices had quieted again and that she'd been staring at Jim Clark, who scowled.

She looked at the men watching her. Somehow she felt calm as she took several steps toward their end of the counter and looked at each of them. "Remember that bomb threat that turned out to be just some prank? Jim told me it was real, had a whole story about how he defused it. Ha. Jim Clark saves the day." Her gaze rested on Jim. "Didn't you think I read the paper?" She took one step closer. "You're a loser. I wouldn't have sex with you if I was the straightest woman on Earth."

She felt their eyes on her back as she walked to Rose.

"What did you say?" Rose asked.

"Nothing. I told him to leave me alone," she said, and pushed past her.

Upstairs, Julia holed up in the bathroom, brushing her teeth. She felt unsettled, knowing they were talking about her downstairs. She wished she hadn't done that, given Jim Clark more cause to hate her. All she wanted to do at the moment was curl up with Rose on the couch in the dark and watch a movie. Difficult conversations could wait until tomorrow. She should have known it meant something that when she was scared or upset, she felt safe with Rose.

But Rose appeared behind her in the bathroom mirror.

"I can't wait for you anymore," she said. "I'm going back to Iowa."

"What? No. No no no." Julia spit and put down her toothbrush. She grabbed Rose's hand. "Why are you saying this? I never said I would be perfect right away. You can't expect me to change overnight."

Rose shook her head. "It doesn't matter. I've reached my end, and I can't wait any longer for you to arrive. Every time you let go of my hand in public or introduce me as your friend, I grow a little more resentful of you. By the time you're able to reach me, I'll hate you so much it won't matter."

"How do you know? What's the purpose of all this, of figuring things out, of changing to become who we are, if it doesn't mean we can be together?"

"You should know the answer to that. And you don't." Rose put Julia's hand to her cheek. "You just don't have it in you, Julia." Then she pulled away. "I'm sorry."

Julia grabbed her arm. "Wait, Rose, please. How can you do this? How can you just decide, so easily, like nothing?"

Rose's face fell, and her eyes shadowed over. "Like nothing? I've thought and cried and written and thought for months, Julia. Months. It's never left me." She walked to the apartment door and closed it gently behind her, leaving Julia alone in the apartment, surrounded by furniture and picture frames and the things she had built up around her.

Downstairs, the men looked at Jim. They didn't hide their disdain.

"Dude," said Steve. He took a step toward the counter, and the others resumed talking. Just like that, Jim was closed out from the group.

He turned on his heel and strode toward the door, his teeth clenched, jaw muscles pulsating in a shame that quickly turned to anger. That was going to be the last time Julia Parnell ever embarrassed him. He almost ran into Julia's girlfriend, who rushed past crying with a suitcase in her hand. She struggled with the drugstore door, then opened it to let in a surprisingly cool rush of air. His hair fluttered as he watched her walk along the sidewalk in front of the store and disappear. Then he turned toward the corner door.

He walked down an aisle and turned right, past the backs of the men at the counter.

At the top of the stairs, Jim stood looking at the sliver of light beneath her door. He thought he heard crying and tried the knob, but it was locked. He knocked. She swung it open, a hopeful smile on her face. And then fear.

He grabbed her throat and pushed her back into the apartment, closing the door behind him. He squeezed, feeling the ropy muscles beneath his fingers. When she started gurgling, he let go and slapped her across the face with a wide-armed swing like a tennis player. "Bitch." He slapped her again as she crouched and tried to block his blows, moving backward. His palm landed on her ear, her hands, the back of her head.

Grabbing her neck again, he pushed her up against the wall, Julia gasping on tiptoes, Jim feeling for the hem of her skirt with his free hand. He lifted the skirt then slid his fingers down into Julia's underwear and up inside her, driving his fingers, knuckles pounding her pubic bone, nails scratching her inside as she tried to wrench her body free. She grunted as she flung her arms out, fists clenched, blind. When she landed a fist on his nose, he yelped, a whiny shriek that angered him.

With one blow to her stomach, Julia landed on all fours. Jim grabbed her hair, pulling her head up, then curled his fingers into a fist. His knuckles struck the side of her face, bruising her brow, her cheek, the corner of her mouth. She cried but it was a tired, gasping cry. Then she stopped.

Her nose and mouth bled. Her skin purpled, and still he punched, pummeling her head with his fist as he hunched over her, until his back could stand it no longer and the muscles along the spine clenched on and squeezed.

He let go of her hair and stepped back, in pain. Julia whimpered once on her hands and knees, her hair falling around her, strands sticking to the blood on her face. Then she crawled, inch by inch, across the carpet to her bedroom. Jim, breathing hard and slumped against the wall, watched as she dragged herself through the doorway, as she disappeared into the darkness and shut the door behind her.

Twenty-Three

O n Thanksgiving Day, Michael went to his uncle's house with his mother. It would be just the three of them. In Minnesota, Michael and his parents always ate an early afternoon dinner together and then joined the neighbors in a game of football near the lake if the weather was nice—above twenty degrees. Those who did not play football skated on the frozen lake. Afterward, they all gathered at one house or another and ate and drank some more, though last Thanksgiving Pike broke his leg jumping over a log on his skates, and Michael accompanied him and Mrs. Mulvey to the hospital.

He and his mother arrived early to help his uncle prepare the food. Anne had told him Uncle Kevin lived in a large house, that he'd planned on marrying someone but now he wasn't going to. He asked, as they walked past the For Sale sign toward the front door, whether Uncle Kevin was moving away.

"No," she said, looking up at the large Tudor. "Just to a different home."

She held a homemade apple pie in one hand as they stepped up to the door. "I suppose we should knock," she said, before rapping a gloved hand on the glass storm door, foggy from the warmth inside. Michael couldn't wait to get out of the chill that had come overnight, which felt so much colder after the warmth of yesterday.

Kevin's table looked like a magazine picture. Even Anne was startled by the large centerpiece of mums and small pumpkins, the bright white china and glimmering silverware, the glass chandelier overhead.

Kevin was sheepish. "They teach you how to make a good table in culinary school." He shuffled them into the kitchen, the counters spread with breads, cheeses, squash, beans, wild rice, water chestnuts, apples, pecans, cranberries, and sweet potatoes. "I just got a bit of everything," said Kevin. "Turkey's already in the oven."

Anne set the pie down and asked for an apron. "I'll chop."

Michael eased onto a kitchen stool and watched his mother. Kevin stood at the counter and cleared his throat.

"Turns out Illinois has some good spots for northern," he said. "I called the DNR. Fox Lake and Sterling Lake are closest, though there are some in the Des Plaines River, too. Not sure we'd want to eat what we catch there, though. There's also a place called Wolf Lake, but that's far."

Michael perked up. "Wolf Lake?"

"Yeah, but it's south of the city. Half of it's in Indiana, even. Probably farther than we want to go."

"No," said Michael. "It sounds perfect."

Kevin nodded. "Alright, then. We'll go Saturday."

"You're here this weekend?"

"Yes. For the first time in a long while."

"Good thing the lakes here haven't started freezing yet. I guess in Minnesota Pike's probably had to stop fishing for a while till the ice is thick enough for drilling."

"Are you telling me I'm going to have to go ice fishing with you?"

"No, we don't have a drill. I always went with Pike. That's what I mean—you're just in time."

The glistening bowls heaped with steaming food were laid on the table. They ate and ate, mashing the salty soft buttery drippings around their tongues until their stomachs rounded, and then they leaned back in their chairs, and Michael relished the smile on his mother's face, on his uncle's face. Surely on his own face. They rubbed their stomachs and licked their greasy fingers and yawned and giggled in their fullness and ate again.

After dinner, Kevin switched on the television. Michael sat, warm, between his mother and uncle on the couch, listening to the hum of the football crowd, feeling the sleepy vibrations of his family's voices as they talked above him.

On Monday, when Michael arrived at school, a substitute teacher sat at Miss Parnell's desk. The young man, pale with rosy cheeks, never stopped smiling as he called out each name for attendance. When he finished, Michael raised his hand.

"Where's Miss Parnell?"

The substitute didn't hesitate. "She's sick. She might be gone for a few days."

On Friday, Michael asked again.

"Still sick," said the substitute.

On Saturday morning, as Michael came down the stairs, his mother sat at the kitchen table reading the newspaper. Warm eggs sat in a skillet, and a carton of milk stood on the table next to two empty glasses and two stacked plates. She'd been staring at the same page for several minutes.

When Michael entered the kitchen, she said, "Honey, come here," and she held Michael's hands as he stood in front of her. "Miss Parnell isn't sick. She's missing."

"Missing what? Where?"

"She's gone, and no one can find her."

"How can no one find her? Where did she go?"

Anne shook her head. "They don't know."

"Who doesn't know?"

"The school, the police. Her parents."

"What about Rose? Did they ask Rose?"

"I'm sure they did, honey."

"Call Rose!"

"Sweetie, the police are taking care of it. They're looking very, very hard."

"What if she's in trouble?" His eyes welled with tears, and he let go of his mother's hands. "What if she needs help?"

Anne rubbed his shoulders and arms, trying to calm him. "Michael, they said she packed some of her things. She might have just decided to leave."

"To go where? Why?"

"I don't know."

"Why would she go somewhere without telling anyone?"

"I wish I knew the answer, Michael."

"Will she come back?"

"I don't know."

He looked at his mother for many seconds while a familiar feeling crept up from his toes, in danger of overcoming the rest of his body. He tried to pull away, but his mother held on to his shoulders, watched him and waited with tears in her eyes for him to speak.

"She left because of me," he said. "She left because I told everyone. I made everyone hate her."

"I don't know why she left, Michael. But I know it's not because of you."

"She wouldn't have had to leave if I didn't say anything."

"If she left because of that, she would have always had to leave, Michael." Anne stroked his cheek. "She might come back."

"She's not coming back." He tried to pull away again, and again she held on.

He wanted to hug and to punch at the same time. His mother saw this, saw his hurt and his anger, and, while continuing to hold onto his arm, reached across the table to a breakfast plate. She grabbed it, held it above their heads, and let it fall to the kitchen floor, where it smashed into a hundred pieces. Then she handed a plate to Michael. He held onto it at first, his big brown eyes watching his mother, before he raised it above his head, slowly, speeding up as his hands came down toward the floor. By the fourth plate, which Anne took from a cabinet, Michael was crying. He let his mother hold him, and they sank onto the floor, surrounded by shards. None of them broke their skin.

Two weeks after Rose left Julia, after she'd returned to their Iowa apartment in the old house on the second floor above Jane, after she'd returned to work and life, when the pain was present but numb and floating, she received a call from her parents in Kansas. They'd just read in the hometown newspaper that Julia was missing.

When Rose hung up, she sat on the kitchen floor and held the phone in her lap. She dialed the operator and was connected with Westway Drugs in Ackerman, Illinois.

"Andy? It's Rose Caldwell."

"Rose. Any news?"

"I just found out. I was calling to ask you."

"No. Nothing."

She called the police.

"Ah, yes. Rose Caldwell." The officer on the other end of the line cleared his throat. "What can I do for you?"

"Don't you want to ask me any questions?"

"Frankly, we didn't see the need. The boys at the drugstore were there all night. They saw you leave, they saw Jim go up, and they saw him come back down. We tracked your car, and we know you went through a toll booth later that night and didn't come back."

"What did Jim Clark say?"

"I've gone through all this with Ms. Parnell's parents."

"Please tell me."

The officer exhaled into the phone. "He left her fine. He admitted to slapping her and causing her nose to bleed. The guys saw him come back down alone and go home about nine thirty. Wife says the same. Andy locked up at midnight. It all checks out."

"Checks out? How do you know he didn't hurt her? Why did he slap her?"

"They had a disagreement. She insulted him—the guys heard it.

Now, if we find her and she wants to press charges, we'll go ahead with assault. As it is, though . . ."

"But he despised her. He threatened her once, in front of his daughter. You can ask her."

"Ms. Caldwell, she packed her bags. Some of her drawers are empty, her toiletries gone. Technically, she's missing. But I think she just up and went."

"Up and went? Where?"

"Wish I could say. Happens more than you'd think. Some people just don't want to be found."

Rose hoped for several days that Julia would come back to her. That she'd left her life in Ackerman to return to Iowa. Every time she opened the door after work, she looked for Julia sitting on the couch or standing at the kitchen counter. Whenever she answered the phone, she anticipated Julia's voice for the first moment. She called Andy every day, just in case. She called the school.

She imagined Julia sitting by a lake in the woods, somewhere secluded and wild and elemental, somewhere she could find whatever it was she needed to start again. To live. When she found it, she'd come back.

She imagined she'd gone to Kansas, back to the very beginning. One day, she even called Julia's parents. Mrs. Parnell was not surprised to hear from her. "No," she said, when Rose asked whether they'd heard from Julia. Just no. No more words, no questions. No string of desperate phrases that indicated she shared any connection with Rose, that they shared any love for the same person. "Please let me know if you do," said Rose. She thought she heard a grunt before Mrs. Parnell hung up.

Then Rose began to dread answering the phone. She didn't want to know.

After several weeks, in one moment—a simple, resounding

moment—as Rose drove her car to work and saw the bare fields stretched out before her, she realized it didn't matter whether Julia left or where she'd gone or whether she'd ever come back. None of it mattered, to her, anymore. It couldn't.

Rose passed work and drove east. For the first hour she rarely blinked, both hands on the steering wheel, elbows taut. She sped by the cornfields and cow pastures, one-story high schools and white clapboard churches with stained glass windows—the kind of windows, Julia told her once, full of a blue so dark and deep it seemed ancient, a blue that made her eyes glaze over and her whole body feel as though it were going through it, into the glass and another time.

Maybe that's where she is, Rose thought, and she chuckled through gathering tears. In a nunnery.

In that moment, she knew she needed to stop. She couldn't go all the way to Ackerman to say goodbye. She pulled over the first chance she could, into the gravel parking lot of a fruit stand abandoned for the winter. She leaned her forehead on the steering wheel, wrapped her arms around herself, and sobbed, the cries rising from deep within. She fell into a rhythm of grief, the sadness humming through her chest and throat, her body rocking in her own arms.

She awoke to silence except for the idling engine. After wiping her cheeks and nose with her hands, she pulled a pen and notepad from her purse. And even though she had nowhere to send it, she wrote a letter, because they always had.

> *Dear Julia,*
> *I love you. Ever since we rescued Tabitha from the stones,*
> *I've loved you. I know you loved me, too, maybe you still do.*
> *But I release you. You're free.*
> *Rose*

She folded the paper and wrote Julia's name on the front. She opened her car door and walked the letter over to the empty counter of the fruit stand, its white paint chipped and peeling. She held the letter to her cheek for several moments, then stuffed it into a slot where the wood counter met the wall of the stand. She made sure it was secure—if only to keep it from flying away aimlessly in the wind—and then walked back to her car. She glanced back once to the white paper visible in the wood; someone would read it some-day. Then she got into her car, pulled onto the road, and headed home.

Twenty-Four

March comes, and with it, Michael's first baseball practice, held in the field near the swimming pool, the same field Michael walked across his first hot days in Ackerman. The sun shines brightly, but the grass and metal benches and baseball bats are cold nonetheless.

He and Sam play catch along the right field line during warm-ups. The field is used for football during the fall. It looks flat, except when he walks on it; then the bumps of clay and dirt under the lawn remind him that this field was leveled once, by bulldozers that cut away the natural fluency of the land. And on top of the gravel-like clods of dirt left behind, someone planted grass seed. Michael looks out across the field and doesn't feel homesick. Something of the opposite, actually. And he remembers that sometimes wolves change territories, too.

Their hands ache, especially when the ball slaps into the palms of their gloves. But before long, their backs are sweating, and Michael's nostrils do not burn dry when he inhales. The coach calls the players in to explain things. Every boy is automatically on the team; there are no tryouts, he says. But he needs to find positions for each boy, so they are asked to run out into the positions of their choice, and he'll hit some balls.

"Infielders, throw to first," the coach calls from home plate. "Outfielders, throw to your cutoff man. You all know what a cutoff man is?" Half the outfielders nod. "Alright, then. Just throw to the infielder closest to you."

Michael is at second, with two boys lined up behind him waiting their turn to catch a grounder. He is ten now, and an inch higher from the infield dirt than he was last year in Minnesota. Sam is at first, the only one. He fields a grounder cleanly and steps on the bag. Then the coach points the bat at Michael and hits a one-hopper to Michael's right. He backhands the ball, plants his foot, and throws a rocket to Sam, who nods at him. Michael knows what this nod means. The two have been talking for three months about this kind of play and all the plays to come. "Durham and Sandberg," they tell each other.

Michael takes his place at the back of the line at second base. The rest of the boys do well, and Michael has hope for the team, if not some worry about his own competition.

But during batting practice, Michael is assured a spot on the starting lineup as soon as the coach discovers he can hit both ways. Michael drives a ball over the shortstop's head, then steps over home plate and repositions himself. The next pitch slaps up dirt on its way to right-center.

The coach smiles from the pitcher's mound. "Did your father teach you that?" he calls.

Michael nods.

"He must have big plans for you."

Michael supposes he does.

After practice, three and a half months after Miss Parnell disappeared, Michael receives a letter dated the afternoon he last saw her, walking on the street with her groceries, though the envelope is postmarked just two days ago.

The Rooms Are Filled

Wednesday, November 23, 1983

Dear Michael,

I wanted to say many things when we met on the sidewalk just now. I could speak only of trivial things and look at you with disappointment. But do you know why? Do you know that I am not angry, Michael, but disappointed that I placed too much responsibility on you? Do you know how much I adore you?

I want to wrap my arms around you and keep you from everything ugly in this world.

Know this: You were my friend. Our relationship was not wrong. It was not ugly. I will always treasure it.

Love,

Miss Parnell

Michael sits in a winter coat on a dry spot on the blacktop driveway, surrounded by rivulets of melting snow making their way from the house to the street. Though the air still feels of winter, the blacktop reflects the warmth of the March sun, and Michael is not cold. He folds the letter closed and lies down, looking up at the blue sky and floating clouds.

Tina is in her yard, and Michael wishes she won't walk over, only because he is so content, but she does.

She sits next to him and picks at the grass that grows along the driveway. They remain, he on his back and she sitting, for several minutes. It becomes comfortable. He notices that her hair is the same gray-brown of the silver maple trunk behind her. He is looking at her hair when a tear falls, sliding off her green eye to her lower lashes and dripping onto her cheek. It travels, leaving bits of itself on the way down to the ground near her bended knee. She makes no effort to wipe it away, and Michael watches as the tear line dries and the peach fuzz on her cheek rises again.

"We're moving," she says. "My dad found a new job."

Michael turns back to the clouds and tries to imagine sitting atop one. How bright and warm it would be. But he cannot keep himself up there, in his mind keeps falling, pulled back down to the earth, to the spot where he lies. He is happy about that.

"I guess I just wanted to tell you," she says. "I'll have to finish sixth grade somewhere else."

Michael has no words but doesn't want her to leave now that she's here. He smiles and she lies down beside him, under the sky.

He grabs her hand and they watch as trains and elephants sail by overhead.

Acknowledgments

Writing a book is a solitary act. Producing one is not. There are many people to thank for this, my first book. Foremost is my husband, Alex, who urged me, an at-home mom, to hire childcare so I could write more. He was also my first reader, the first one to tell me I had something.

My sister, Katie, has been a relentless cheerleader for me, almost to an embarrassing degree. She was my second reader and read all the way to the end. My brother, Eric, wrote lovely poems and stories as a child, and I wanted to emulate him. It's because of him that I write.

It's also because of my mother, Barbara, who raised me to assume that with hard work I could do anything I wanted, and my father, Dave, who read to me and passed on his love of literature and story-telling. He was my first fan.

In high school, I showed my stepfather, Pat, a piece of my prose, which I thought was filled with lovely words. He read it, looked up at me, and said, "What's the point? There has to be a point." Sage advice.

Support urges the writer onward, and I received bucketfuls, so thank you to the Nulls, Vealitzeks, Kinders, and AP et al., and to some of my greatest advocates: Susan, Kelly, Heather, Melanie, Ginny, Michelle, and Danielle, who told me to "Send it up to the Universe and have a blast." I'm also grateful for the readers of my blog, the first people to read my writing of their own volition.

Many thanks to my critique group—Amy Herlihy, Elizabeth Campbell Frey, and Nancy Cohn. Editor Susan Dalsimer believed in my book early on and helped make it better, richer, fuller. Ditto Mary Breaden, who added layers to the layers already there. The final product wouldn't be what it is without these people.

The wonderful writers of She Writes, the first online community I ever joined, helped me feel comfortable in the skin of a "writer" and answered all my newbie questions. Melanie Conklin polished my synopsis; her organization inspires me.

My fellow readers and writers at Great New Books—Jennifer Lyn King, Hallie Sawyer, Nina Badzin, Lindsey Mead, and Stacey Loscalzo—are friends, supporters, and constant sources of inspiration.

And, of course, thank you to everyone at She Writes Press, especially Brooke Warner and Kamy Wicoff, who created a fantastic new business model in the middle of a changing industry.

As for the two little people to whom this book is dedicated, I consider my life a success for the fortune of being their mother.

About the Author

Jessica Null Vealitzek was born and raised northwest of Chicago, where she still lives with her husband and two children. This is her first novel.

SELECTED TITLES FROM SHE WRITES PRESS

She Writes Press is an independent publishing company founded to serve women writers everywhere.
Visit us at www.shewritespress.com.

The Belief in Angels by J. Dylan Yates
$16.95, 978-1-938314-64-3

From the Majdonek death camp to a volatile hippie household on the East Coast, this narrative of tragedy, survival, and hope spans more than fifty years, from the 1920s to the 1970s.

Hysterical: Anna Freud's Story by Rebecca Coffey
$18.95, 978-1-938314-42-1

An irreverent, fictionalized exploration of the seemingly contradictory life of Anna Freud—told from her point of view.

Our Love Could Light the World by Anne Leigh Parrish
$15.95, 978-1-938314-44-5

Twelve stories depicting a dysfunctional and chaotic—yet lovable—family that has to band together in order to survive.

Beautiful Garbage by Jill DiDonato
$16.95, 978-1-938314-01-8

Talented but troubled young artist Jodi Plum leaves suburbia for the excitement of the city—and is soon swept up in the sexual politics and downtown art scene of 1980s New York.

Cleans Up Nicely by Linda Dahl
$16.95, 978-1-938314-38-4

The story of one gifted young woman's path from self-destruction to self-knowledge, set in mid-1970s Manhattan.

Bittersweet Manor by Tory McCagg
$16.95, 978-1-938314-56-8

A chronicle of three generations of love, manipulation, entitlement, and disappointed expectations in an upper-middle class New England family.

www.ingramcontent.com/pod-product-compliance
Lightning Source LLC
Chambersburg PA
CBHW032336180125
20237CB00009B/100

* 9 7 8 1 9 3 8 3 1 4 5 8 2 *